A Rewarding Favor . . .

Grandmother Otero nodded. "When Catarina told me you were wanting to learn Portuguese because you were going to Lisbon, I thought you might be able to help my friend Frau Rilke."

"I hope we can," Frank said. He turned to Frau Rilke. "What is it you want us to do?"

Frau Rilke took in a deep breath and let it out slowly. "In 1943 my father buried a suitcase full of gold bars in the garden of our house in Lisbon."

Frank and Joe looked at each other, shocked.

Frau Rilke leaned close to them. "When you're in Lisbon, I want you to go to the house, dig up the gold, and bring it back to me. My children and their families are short of money, and this gold would help them tremendously. If you do this for me, I'll give each of you a gold bar."

The Hardy Boys Mystery Stories

Available from ALADDIN Paperbacks

THE **HARDY BOYS**®

#182

THE SECRET OF THE SOLDIER'S GOLD

FRANKLIN W. DIXON

Aladdin Paperbacks
New York London Toronto Sydney

This book is a work of fiction. Any references to historical events,
real people, or real locales are used fictitiously. Other names, characters, places,
and incidents are the product of the author's imagination,
and any resemblance to actual events or locales or persons, living or dead,
is entirely coincidental.

First Aladdin Paperbacks edition December 2003
Copyright © 2003 by Simon & Schuster, Inc.

ALADDIN PAPERBACKS
An imprint of Simon & Schuster
Children's Publishing Division
1230 Avenue of the Americas
New York, NY 10020

The text of this book was set in New Caledonia.

Printed in the United States of America
8 10 9

THE HARDY BOYS MYSTERY STORIES is a trademark of Simon & Schuster, Inc.

THE HARDY BOYS and colophon are registered trademarks of Simon & Schuster, Inc.

Library of Congress Control Number 2003103454

ISBN 0-689-85885-X

1209 OFF

Contents

THE SECRET OF THE
SOLDIER'S GOLD

1 Frau Rilke's Strange Story

Eighteen-year-old Frank Hardy stretched his tall frame above the crowd of students who were changing classes at Bayport High School. "I don't see her," he said to his brother, Joe. Frank combed his fingers through his dark brown hair in frustration. "I'm going to be late for Spanish. Are you sure Catarina has a class this hour in one of these rooms?"

"She's a freshman, Frank. Remember?" Joe said. "All of the freshman classes are in this part of the building." He scanned the crowd with his blue eyes. Finally he spotted her. "There she is!" he shouted.

Catarina Otero suddenly noticed the Hardy boys and flashed a brilliant smile. "Frank! Joe!" she called. "Over here!"

The Hardys forced their way through the crowd

to the side of the hall where Catarina had taken refuge.

"Now what is this important question you want to ask me?" Catarina asked.

"Do you still want to teach me some Portuguese?" Joe said.

Catarina raised an eyebrow. "Well, sure, Joe, but what changed your mind? The last time I offered, you said you weren't interested."

"We're going to Portugal during the winter break," Frank said. "Dad's been invited by a friend in the Lisbon Police Department, Inspector Manuel Oliveira." Fenton Hardy, the boys' father, was a world-famous detective whose expertise was often sought after.

Catarina's eyes widened. "Oh, you guys are so lucky! Sure, I'll be glad to teach you some Portuguese. In fact, why don't you come to my birthday party tomorrow afternoon? Many members of my family will be there, which means there will be a lot of people speaking Portuguese. You can learn by total immersion."

"Hey—great idea!" Joe said.

"Thanks, Catarina," Frank said.

As the Hardy boys headed back toward their part of the building Joe said, "I hope Iola and Callie don't get mad because we're going to a party hosted by a freshman girl."

Frank grinned. "I'll talk to Callie and you can talk to Iola," he said. "We'll just tell them it's business."

Joe laughed. "Yeah, right! I'm sure they'll believe that," he said.

Iola was the sister of Chet Morton, one of the boys' best friends. She and Callie Shaw were two of the most popular girls in school and often spent time with Frank and Joe.

When Frank reached his math class, he said, "I'm glad you remembered Catarina's offer to teach you Portuguese, Joe. Who knows? We may be able to help the Lisbon police too."

"Yeah, that's what I was thinking," Joe said. "See you after school!"

As Joe took his seat in the third row next to the window he remembered a World War II movie he had seen on television during the last week. It was set in Lisbon, and the story had involved lots of spies. The city had been portrayed as a hotbed of criminal activity. Who knew—Lisbon might be full of mysteries for them to solve.

"Mama, this is Frank and Joe Hardy. They're friends of mine from school," Catarina said.

"Welcome to our house," Mrs. Otero said. "I'm so happy you could come to Catarina's birthday party."

"Thank you, Mrs. Otero," Frank said. "We're delighted to be here."

Frank and Joe are going to Lisbon next week," Catarina explained. "They want to learn some Portuguese and I'm going to teach them."

"Oh, that's wonderful! I wish I were going with you," Mrs. Otero said. She looked around the room. "Catarina, these young men look starved. You should get them some food."

"Okay, Mama," Catarina said.

Mrs. Otero patted Frank and Joe on the arms. "I need to check on the other guests," she said. "Thank you again for coming." With that she began circulating through the room.

Catarina smiled. "My birthday party may not be what you expected. This one is actually just going to be attended by my family," she said. "Tonight, though, I'll have some of my girlfriends from school over. *That* will be the real party!"

"I think this is a great custom, Catarina," Joe said. "Two birthday parties in one day. Can't really go wrong!"

"Anyway, as I said, almost everyone here will be speaking Portuguese. You'll have a chance to hear it and then I'll translate for you," Catarina said. "It'll be almost like you're already in Lisbon."

"Sort of a trial run," Frank said.

Catarina nodded.

For the next several minutes the teens made their way around the room as unobtrusively as possible, listening in on conversations and eating from the plate of party snacks that Catarina had made for them. Every once in a while, Catarina would introduce Frank and Joe to someone new. Everyone the boys met switched easily from Portuguese to English and back again.

Finally, just before they reached the last group, Catarina said, "I've been saving my grandmother for last."

"We'd love to meet her," Frank said.

Earlier Frank had noticed two elderly women seated together in a corner of the room and deduced, mostly from the deference the women had been shown, that they must be family matriarchs. They were both dressed in black from head to toe, and they had their steel-gray hair pinned up in knots on top of their heads.

Joe had noticed them too and was curious about who they were. "Which one of them is your grandmother?" he asked.

"The one on the right is Grandmother Otero, my father's mother," Catarina said. "The woman with her is Frau Rilke, Grandmother Otero's good friend who lives here in Bayport."

"*Frau* Rilke? That's German, right?" Frank asked.

Catarina nodded. "Grandmother Otero says that Frau Rilke lived in Lisbon for several years during World War II," she explained. "Grandmother Otero

5

ws all about your famous father and the mysteries e two of you have solved. When I told her that you were coming to my party so I could teach you some Portuguese, she asked me if you could help her friend Frau Rilke with a problem. I didn't know what to tell her. . . ."

"Oh, we're always being asked to solve cases," Joe said. "It's no big deal."

"We'll be glad to talk to Frau Rilke," Frank said. "Don't worry about it."

Frank could see the immediate relief on Catarina's face. She obviously had been concerned about it.

"Grandmother Otero!" Catarina called to the woman. "I'd like to introduce Frank and Joe Hardy. They're my friends from school."

Grandmother Otero looked up, blinked, and suddenly gave them a big smile. "Forgive me for not standing up. Arthritis." She turned and nodded at Frau Rilke. "This is my dear friend, Brigette Rilke."

Frau Rilke nodded at them and managed a smile, although it was easy for Frank to see that she was not feeling very happy. *Well,* he thought, *if Joe and I can solve her problem, then maybe that will change.*

"Catarina, dear, did you tell your friends about . . ." Grandmother Otero stopped herself, not knowing, Joe guessed, whether she should go any further.

"Yes, Grandmother," Catarina said. "They're happy to do what they can to help."

At that moment Frau Rilke let out a sob and tears streamed down her cheeks. "Oh, thank you, thank you," she managed to say.

Catarina looked a little embarrassed. "Joe," she said, "will you help me pull up some chairs so we can all talk more comfortably?"

Joe, now somewhat puzzled by Frau Rilke's emotional outburst, had begun to wonder about the magnitude of the case they had agreed to solve.

Joe helped Catarina pull three chairs to Grandmother Otero and Frau Rilke. The three teens sat down.

"Everyone in Bayport knows how important your father is. He has helped many, many people," Grandmother Otero began. "And his sons are almost just as famous."

Frank and Joe smiled at her.

"Well, we think it's important for people to use their talents to help people however they can," Frank said.

"We like solving mysteries for people," Joe added.

Grandmother Otero nodded. "That's why, when Catarina told me you were wanting to learn Portuguese because you were going to Lisbon, I thought you might be able to help my friend Frau Rilke."

"I hope we can," Frank said. He turned to Frau Rilke. "What is it you want us to do?"

Frau Rilke took in a deep breath and let it out slowly. "In 1943 my father buried a suitcase full of gold bars in the garden of our house in Lisbon."

Frank and Joe looked at each other, shocked.

Frau Rilke leaned close to them. "When you're in Lisbon, I want you to go to the house, dig up the gold, and bring it back to me. My children and their families are short of money, and this gold would help them tremendously. If you do this for me, I'll give each of you a gold bar."

2 The Suitcase Full of Gold

Frank was stunned by what he had just heard. He looked at Joe, his eyes conveying what his mouth couldn't say: *What in the world have we gotten ourselves into? Is Frau Rilke serious?*

Joe got the message. "Would that be legal, Frau Rilke?" he said. "I'm not sure the Portuguese authorities would let us do something like that."

Frau Rilke's lower lip trembled. "I don't want you to break the law, but . . ."

"Oh, no!" Grandmother Otero interjected. "Brigette would never expect you to do something like that."

Frau Rilke dabbed at her eyes with an embroidered linen handkerchief. "You boys have solved so many mysteries in Bayport that I was just sure you could figure out some solution to this," she said. "That gold belongs to my family and we need it now in order to survive."

"Please just listen to her story," Grandmother Otero said. "I beg of you."

"Grandmother, if Frank and Joe don't think—," Catarina started to say, but Joe interrupted her.

"No, no, Catarina, it's okay," Joe said. He looked at Frank. "It won't hurt to hear the whole story. Who knows? We might be able to bring the gold back without getting into trouble."

"We can't promise anything, Frau Rilke," Frank added, "but, as Joe said, we'll be glad to help if we can."

"That's all I ask," Frau Rilke said.

"Catarina, this may take a few minutes, so why don't you go get the boys more food?" Grandmother Otero said. "And if you wouldn't mind, dear, could you also bring a fresh pot of coffee for Brigette and me?"

"Of course, Grandmother. I've forgotten my manners," Catarina said. She looked at Frank and Joe. "I'll bring back some Portuguese specialties so that you can start getting used to the food. Sound good?"

"That sounds *great* to me," Joe said.

Frank nodded his agreement and turned to Frau Rilke. "I've read a lot of stories about what happened during World War II, but I've never actually talked to anybody who experienced it firsthand."

"It was a terrible time," Frau Rilke began, her voice breaking. "We lost everything."

Grandmother Otero took her hand. "It's okay, Brigette," she said. "I'm here."

Frau Rilke dabbed at her eyes again. "My family and I used to live in Berlin, Germany. That's where I was born. Our name was Fleissner and my father was a popular man. He and my mother loved Germany—they thought of themselves as true Germans. But by 1941 life had become very difficult for us. With the help of friends we were able to escape to Portugal, but we had to leave all of our belongings behind. My family was quite wealthy, but we arrived in Lisbon with only the clothes on our backs and what we had been able to stuff in our pockets."

"That's terrible," Joe said. He was trying to imagine what it would be like to leave his house and everything he owned, and never be able to return.

"Oh, it was," Frau Rilke said. "I cried and cried."

"Why did you go to Portugal?" Frank asked.

"My father didn't want to leave Europe, and Portugal was politically neutral. He thought we'd be safe there. He also knew other German families who had gone to Portugal before the war started, and he was hoping to make contact with them," Frau Rilke said. "My mother wanted us to go to

Canada or the United States. She knew that ships still sailed from Lisbon to those countries, and she was hoping to convince my father that ultimately, that was what we should do."

Catarina arrived with a fresh pot of coffee and two plates of food. After she served her grandmother and Frau Rilke, she told Frank and Joe the Portuguese names of all the food on their plates and made them repeat the words back to her. "Not bad," she said when the boys were finished. "I think you're going to do very well in Lisbon."

"Right," Joe said. "If we only have to order food, then we'll have no problem!"

Joe's joke broke the tension. Everyone laughed.

When Catarina started to leave, Joe said, "Don't go. Join us! This is interesting." He moved his chair over to make room for her.

Catarina pulled up a chair and sat between Joe and Frank.

"Please continue, Brigette," Grandmother Otero said.

"After we arrived in Lisbon, several German families we had managed to contact helped us get settled," Frau Rilke said. "My father was able to obtain work and we eventually moved into our own house. Adjusting to our new lives was hard, but we kept faith that life would return to normal for us again and that the rest of the world would return to normal too." Frau Rilke shook her head and gave them a sad smile. "We actually thought back then that one day we could return to our home in Germany and that things would be exactly as they used to be."

Grandmother Otero patted her friend's hand. "That is what we all wish from time to time, Brigette," she said, "that we can bring back the happier times in our lives."

Frau Rilke nodded. "One day, in 1943, we received a visit from Heinz-Erich Lüdemann, the son of family friends in Berlin. He had been an officer in the German Army, but Heinz's father, an important businessman, was accused of plotting against Hitler—and suddenly Heinz's entire family and all their possessions disappeared. Heinz received the news while his unit was in the south of France. At that time his unit had been transporting trucks of gold bars to different Atlantic ports to be shipped to South America. Some of the Nazi High Command could already see the writing on the wall—that they'd be defeated—and by shipping the gold, they were hoping to reestablish themselves in Argentina and Paraguay.

"Anyway, some of his friends warned him that the Gestapo, the dreaded German secret police, planned to arrest him. So he decided to take an amount of gold that he thought would equal the fortune the Nazis had taken from his family and from ours. He put the gold bars in a metal suitcase and brought it with him to Lisbon. Heinz told my father that half of the gold belonged to him and that we could use it to rebuild our lives. He planned to use his half to finance missions back to Germany to help defeat the Nazis.

"For safekeeping my father decided to bury the suitcase in the backyard garden of our house in Lisbon. We always referred to this garden as our *park*."

"Why was that?" Joe asked.

"Well, the custom started while we were still in Berlin," Frau Rilke said. "Hitler said that Jews could no longer go to public parks, so we just started sitting in our garden and telling everyone that we were sitting in the park." She smiled. "It made us feel better. With our friends, we'd always ask, 'Do you want to go to the park?' The answer, of course, would be, 'Yes!' We'd then go to the backyard garden of someone's house and sit in the 'park.'"

"What a terrible thing to happen," Frank said, clearly referring to the whole story.

"It was, but the whole experience made us strong," Frau Rilke said. "When challenged, the human mind can come up with solutions to the most impossible problems."

"So even after you moved to Lisbon, you still called

14

your backyard garden the park?" Catarina asked.

Frau Rilke nodded. "It was a difficult habit to break," she said, "but because of that, I'm hoping the gold is still there."

"What do you mean?" Joe asked.

"Well, one day my father went to meet Heinz in central Lisbon to discuss a business proposition. Just as my father got there he witnessed Heinz's kidnapping by men whom he knew were Gestapo. There was nothing my father could do but watch in horror. He was sure that Heinz would be taken back to Germany and executed.

"By the time my father got back to our house, he was so scared that he could hardly talk. He knew the same thing that happened to Heinz could easily happen to us. So he immediately obtained passage for us on the next ship to the United States. He decided that it was too dangerous to take the gold.

"Since the Gestapo had ways of getting information out of people, my father believed that in the end Heinz would reveal not only our whereabouts but also the location of the suitcase full of gold bars. My father's hope, though, was that Heinz would say the gold was buried in the *park*." Frau Rilke picked up her purse, opened it, and took out a piece of paper. She handed it to Frank. "I've drawn a map of the backyard of what used to be our house in Lisbon," she said. "The X marks the spot where my father buried the suitcase of gold bars."

Frank and Joe studied the map together.

"Well, this will certainly be helpful," Joe said.

"So you'll help me?" Frau Rilke asked expectantly.

"We'll need to talk to our father first," Frank said, "but Joe and I will do all we can to help you."

"Does anyone else besides your immediate family and the people in your old circle of friends know about the gold?" Joe asked.

Frau Rilke started to shake her head but stopped suddenly. "Well, yes—but it would not be important after all of these years."

"What do you mean?" Catarina asked.

"I had a very dear friend in Lisbon. She was a Portuguese girl who lived across the street from us. Rosa Santos was her name. I told her about the gold. You know how children are," Frau Rilke said. "My parents said never to mention anything about the treasure to anyone, but Rosa and I were always making up stories for each other. So I told her my father had buried a suitcase full of gold bars in the park. I'm not sure if she believed me or not."

Frank and Joe looked at each other.

"Are you sure you said 'in the park' and not 'in our garden'?" Joe asked.

Frau Rilke thought for a moment. "No—I'm *not* really sure," she said. "It was just a game and I suppose I wanted to brag a bit to Rosa. She was always bragging to me about things her father did."

This could certainly complicate matters, Frank thought. If Frau Rilke had indeed told Rosa that the suitcase of gold bars was buried in her backyard, then after Frau Rilke and her family left, Rosa could have convinced somebody to dig for the gold.

Joe looked at his watch. "We should be going," he said. "Dad has some chores he wants us to do."

"Then you will help me?" Frau Rilke asked.

"Yes, we'll do all we can," Frank told her again.

"You are such wonderful young men," Grandmother Otero said. "I am so glad you are friends with Catarina."

Frank and Joe said their good-byes, thanked Catarina's parents for their hospitality, and followed Catarina to the door.

"Well, you didn't learn as much Portuguese as I'd hoped today," she said. "I'm sorry."

"But we heard a very interesting story," Joe said.

"Do you think that's all it is?" Catarina asked. "A story?"

"No, I believe it happened. In fact, I've heard similar stories about families who lived through World War II," Frank said. "The problem is that this all happened such a long time ago, and somebody could have already found the gold."

"We'll talk to our dad about it," Joe said. "I'll call you tonight."

"Okay," Catarina said. "And I'll make a list of some of the most important Portuguese phrases to remember."

"Great!" Joe said.

"You'd better add to that list something like, 'We're looking for a suitcase full of gold bars,'" Frank said, smirking.

3 Friends Never Forget

When Frank and Joe arrived back at their house, their father was just coming out of his study.

"How was the birthday party, boys?" Mr. Hardy asked. "Did you learn a lot of Portuguese?"

"No, but we heard a really strange story, Dad," Frank said. "We need to talk to you about it."

Fenton Hardy raised an eyebrow. "Oh?"

Joe nodded. "A friend of Catarina's grandmother's, Frau Rilke, asked us to bring back a suitcase of gold bars from Lisbon. Her father buried the suitcase in the garden of their house during World War II."

Mr. Hardy gave them an astonished look and glanced down at his watch. "Well, I'm supposed to meet Chief Collig at police headquarters in twenty minutes, but it won't hurt if I'm a few minutes late," he said. "Come on into my study—I want to hear Frau Rilke's story."

After hearing all about the gold and the relocation of Frau Rilke's family, Fenton Hardy spoke. "Fascinating. I knew things like that happened, but I've never known anyone who actually experienced it."

"That's exactly what I thought too," Frank said.

"Can we help her, Dad?" Joe said. "I think she's really counting on us."

"Well, I'm not sure. We'll just have to test the waters once we get to Lisbon. I'll talk to my friends in the Lisbon Police Department about the best way to proceed. I believe that the German people still have a right to claim anything that was taken from them during that time," Mr. Hardy said, looking at Frank and Joe. "Right now I wouldn't say a word about this to anyone, though. In fact, I think it would be a good idea if one of you called Catarina and told her to relay that to her grandmother and Frau Rilke."

Two days later the Hardy family—including Aunt Gertrude—boarded a flight from New York to Portugal. After six hours and forty minutes in the air, they landed at Lisbon's Portela Airport.

Inspector Oliveira met them just outside customs. "You may have to shed your coats," he said. "It's eighteen degrees outside."

"Oh, it's freezing!" Aunt Gertrude said. "Why would I want to take off my coat?"

20

"Oh no, I'm sorry. That's eighteen degrees *Celsius*," Inspector Oliveira said, smiling. "That's about . . . hmm . . . sixty-five degrees Fahrenheit."

"Oh my, that sounds nice," Mrs. Hardy said. "Much warmer than Bayport."

"If this weather keeps up, and maybe gets a little warmer, I'm going to be spending a lot of time on the beach," Joe said to Frank. "I need to work on my tan."

"Great idea, Joe," Frank agreed. "Right after we take care of business, though."

On the ride to the Hotel Lisboa Plaza in Lisbon, Inspector Oliveira pointed out some of the landmarks. From time to time Frank and Joe would listen, but they were really thinking about looking for Frau Rilke's gold. On the flight from New York they had continued to discuss the matter with their father. Together they had decided that before they talked to the Portuguese authorities Frank and Joe would check out where Frau Rilke's family had lived. They first had to see if the house and the garden were still there.

"For all we know, the whole place could be a parking lot now," Frank had suggested on the plane.

Mr. Hardy had agreed.

Joe now had a map of metropolitan Lisbon spread out on his lap and he and Frank were studying it. The address of Frau Rilke's old house was 22 Rua de Francisco de Almeida. Joe could see

21

that it was actually in Belém, a suburb of Lisbon.

"That's a famous place, Belém," Frank said. "Vasco da Gama set sail for India from there in 1497."

"These red lines represent tram tracks," Joe said. He traced one of the lines from their hotel to Belém. "Getting there should be easy."

The closer they got to the central part of Lisbon, the heavier and slower the traffic became. Joe folded up the map and looked out the window just as Inspector Oliveira said, "See those young men over there in front of that store? If the government doesn't put a stop to their activities, Portugal is going to have some serious problems."

"What do you mean?" Frank asked.

"They're members of a local fascist group," Inspector Oliveira replied. "We have several groups like this in Portugal, but so do almost all of the other countries in Europe. Unfortunately they're cropping up all over the world these days. I just wish any of the fascists in Lisbon would do something illegal so we could lock them up in prison."

Joe leaned over to Frank. "Does he mean Nazis?" he whispered.

"They probably don't call themselves that," Frank whispered back, "but yeah, I'm pretty sure that's what he means."

"I understand how you feel, Manuel," Fenton Hardy said, "but in a democracy, such things just have to be tolerated."

Inspector Oliveira shrugged. It was obvious to Frank that he didn't want to get into an argument over the matter with their father.

"I guess none of us should really be surprised, since fascism probably never died out entirely after World War II," Inspector Oliveira said. "Dr. Salazar ruled Portugal from 1932 until 1968, and he was a supporter of Hitler's Germany and Franco's Spain."

"That must have been a very difficult time for everyone," Frank said.

"It was. Well, here's your hotel," Inspector Oliveira said. "I think you'll find it quite comfortable."

"It looks lovely," Mrs. Hardy said.

"That's a nice little park across the street too," Aunt Gertrude added, pointing out the window. "It'll be a good place to get some fresh air."

"I plan to get my fresh air on the beach, as soon as possible!" Joe said.

As it turned out, getting to where Frau Rilke had once lived wasn't very easy. After the Hardys checked in to their hotel and unpacked, Frank and Joe stopped by a newsstand just off the lobby and picked up a more detailed tramline map. Joe discovered that they would have to change trams a couple of times. With Frank navigating, though, the trip went without a hitch.

"This thing is proving to be much simpler than I'd thought it would be," Joe said.

"Well, so far it is," Frank said. "Remember, though, our mission's just begun."

When they finally arrived at 22 Rua de Francisco de Almeida, Joe said, "I think I might have spoken too soon."

The house was more a mansion than a house. A high, wrought-iron fence topped with dangerous-looking spikes surrounded the huge backyard. Guard dogs patrolled the perimeter of the property inside the fence.

"I wonder who lives here now?" Joe whispered.

Frank shrugged. "It must be somebody important," he said. He shook his head in dismay. "I certainly never expected this."

"Me neither," Joe said. "How do we talk to the person who lives inside?"

"Well, I guess we just walk up to the front door and ring the bell," Frank suggested, starting toward the house.

Frank had taken only a couple of steps when a guard with a machine gun jumped out from behind a shrub.

"*O que quer?*" he demanded in Portuguese.

"I don't remember learning that from Catarina," Joe said.

"What do you want?" the guard repeated in English.

"We're from the United States," Frank said. "A friend of ours lived here in 1943."

"We need to talk to the person who lives here now," Joe added. "It's kind of complicated, but it's very important to our friend."

The guard looked, Frank thought, as if he were trying to translate what they had just said and make some sense of it. After a minute he said, "Do you have any identification?" He positioned his machine gun so that it was pointing directly at them.

"Here," Frank said. He offered his passport to the guard.

The guard took it, studied it carefully for a moment, and then returned it.

"You?" the guard said to Joe. "Let me see your passport."

Joe handed over his passport, and the guard studied it just as carefully as he had studied Frank's.

Finally satisfied that neither Frank nor Joe meant harm to whoever lived in this house, the guard said, "Senhora Bragança is here now. You may ring the bell."

Frank and Joe walked up the steps to the porch. Behind them they heard a clicking sound, and they knew that the guard still had his machine gun aimed at them.

Frank pushed a button and they heard a chiming inside the house. Within a few seconds the front door opened, revealing an elderly woman.

"We're Frank and Joe Hardy, and we're from the United States," Frank said. "Would you please tell

Senhora Bragança that we'd like to speak to her?"

"I'm Maria Bragança," the woman said. "What is it that you wish?"

For just a few seconds both Frank and Joe were taken aback. After their encounter with the guard, it hadn't occurred to them that Senhora Bragança would actually open the door herself. *She must have been watching through the window,* Joe thought. *Probably she had already been informed by another guard that two Americans wanted to talk to her.*

"We're here on behalf of the woman who used to live in this house back in 1943. Her name is Brigette Rilke, but her last name was Fleissner back then," he said. "She sent us on a very important mission to bring back something that belongs to her family."

Maria Bragança's face turned pale. "Leave at once!" she shouted at them. "Never come back to this house!" With that, Senhora Bragança slammed the door in their faces.

Frank and Joe looked at each other.

"I think we struck a nerve," Joe said. "She knew exactly what we're looking for, didn't she? And we didn't even mention the gold."

"I think so," Frank agreed.

Joe turned around and looked at the guard who was now staring coldly at them. "Now what?" he whispered to Frank.

"Well, we can't just stand here—that's for sure," Frank said.

The Hardy boys started back down the steps.

The guard followed them with the barrel of his gun.

Just as Frank and Joe reached the street the guard was distracted by an approaching automobile. A large metal gate at the side of the house swung open and the automobile drove through it. The guard stood at the gate to make sure that it closed again, and then he resumed his duties near the shrubs at the front of the house.

Out of the corner of one eye Frank watched as people climbed out of the automobile. He saw two women dressed in uniforms—they looked like they might have been maids. Frank noted the time on his watch.

"Senhora Bragança must be really wealthy to have so many people working for her," Joe said.

Frank stopped. "Maybe that's it, Joe—maybe that's the reason she looked so frightened when we mentioned Frau Rilke," he said. "What if *she* found the suitcase with the gold bars? That could be the source of her fortune."

"You're right, Frank," Joe said. "And if that's the case, there's probably nothing we can do about getting the gold back."

Frank started walking down the sidewalk, away

from Senhora Bragança's house. "This whole neighborhood is suspicious," he whispered. "There's a woman watching us from that house across the street. I think we should get out of here."

Joe stopped. "Wait a minute, Frank. Frau Rilke said the only other person she had told about the suitcase was a little girl who lived across the street," he said. "Maybe that woman who's looking at us knows something about Frau Rilke's friend. Let's go and talk to her."

4 Trapped!

Just as Frank and Joe started toward the front door
of the house across the street, the woman who had
been watching them moved away from the window.

Frank stopped, but Joe continued walking.

"We've come this far, Frank—I think this is
worth a try," Joe said. "Maybe she thinks we're
door-to-door salesmen, and that's why she left the
window?"

"Maybe—okay," Frank said. He hurried to catch
up with Joe.

When they reached the front door, Joe rang the
bell. Both boys were surprised when the woman
who had been watching them immediately opened
the door and looked right at them.

"*Sim?*" she said.

"Fala inglês?" Joe asked.

"Sim," the woman said. "Yes, I speak English."

"We're Frank and Joe Hardy," Joe said. He nodded across the street to Senhora Bragança's house. "A friend of ours in the United States used to live over there when she was a little girl, and we . . ."

Frank noticed the woman giving them a puzzled look.

"Well, Frau Rilke is really a friend of a friend," he explained.

The woman nodded.

"When she lived here back in 1943, her name was Brigette Fleissner," Joe said. "She . . ."

The woman gasped. "Brigette! My dear friend, Brigette!"

Frank and Joe looked at each other, surprised.

"Are you Rosa Santos?" Frank asked.

"Yes, yes I am. My married name, however, is de Feira," Senhora de Feira said. "This was my childhood home. I inherited it from my parents after they died." She stood aside. "Oh, please come in and tell me all about Brigette! This is such a wonderful surprise."

Joe couldn't believe their luck. Maybe his initial feeling on their way to Senhora Bragança's house—that this mission would be easier than they had thought—had been on target after all.

Frank, on the other hand, was having second thoughts. As Senhora de Feira led them into the interior of her house he felt a chill—not just from the unusually cold air around him, but from the house itself. Very little light entered the house, and the dark, heavy furniture created a very somber setting. This was not the house of very happy people, Frank observed to himself.

Finally in the back of the house they reached a room with a huge fireplace, which, though full of burning logs, gave off very little warmth until Frank and Joe were standing right in front of it. The teens both wondered why the woman had a fire burning with such nice weather outside, but they let it go.

Senhora de Feira sat in a straight-backed side chair on the left of the fireplace. A small, round reading table, topped by an ornate lamp, stood to the right of the chair. "I'm sorry if the house seems chilly to you," she apologized. "This house is always a bit cold."

"It's fine," Frank said hurriedly, realizing his and Joe's slightly cautious behavior might have seemed rude to Senhora de Feira. "This is just such a beautiful fireplace—I couldn't resist looking at it more closely."

"Thank you. Won't you please join me?" Senhora de Feira motioned to a sofa that faced her chair. "I'll have some good Portuguese coffee sent in." She pulled a cord at the side of the table. "Actually, we use Brazilian coffee, but Brazil was settled by the Portuguese—as I'm sure you know—so I still refer to it as Portuguese coffee."

Senhora de Feira smiled, though Frank thought her smile seemed forced. She then turned to face the fire, and for several moments she seemed totally lost in her own thoughts.

Frank was beginning to feel even more uncomfortable than before, and was thinking that he and Joe should come up with an excuse to leave, but he knew that if they were going to succeed in finding Frau Rilke's suitcase with the gold bars, they'd probably need Senhora de Feira's help. He took a deep breath and tried to calm down.

For once in his life Joe had nothing to say either, so the three of them sat in silence for a few minutes, listening to the crackling fire. Finally a maid walked in with the coffee and broke the quiet.

The arrival of the coffee seemed to break Senhora de Feira's trance. "Oh, wonderful, wonderful!" she said.

The maid set the coffee service on a buffet, poured three small cups of coffee, and served everyone.

"*Un garoto*," Senhora de Feira said. "With milk. I hope you don't mind. It's a wonderful treat, I think."

"It looks delicious," Frank said.

Joe nodded.

They both took a couple of sips. It was much

stronger than either one of them liked, but they were determined to finish it to be polite.

"Now then, tell me all about my dear Brigette," Senhora de Feira said. "Please don't leave anything out."

Joe started the story. He told her how they had asked Catarina Otero to teach them some Portuguese and how when they went to her birthday party to hear some of the language being spoken, they had heard Frau Rilke's story.

"We told her we'd try to find the suitcase with the gold bars so she could help her family through their financial problems," Frank finished. "That's why we . . ."

"Ah, yes, the suitcase with the gold bars," Senhora de Feira said, her eyes gleaming. "I remember that story as if Brigette had told it to me yesterday." She paused for several seconds, turned to stare at the fireplace, then turned back to look at the Hardys. "Her father buried it in a park, but there are so many parks in Lisbon that it would be impossible to dig them all up." She smiled. "Did she perhaps tell you in which park we—I mean, *you*—should look?"

The question took Joe by surprise. He glanced over at Frank, who was still looking at Senhora de Feira. "Well, no, she didn't," he said. "I think—"

"As a matter of fact," Frank interrupted him, "we

were sort of hoping that you might have an idea about which park we should check out."

Senhora de Feira's face sagged noticeably. It was obvious to Joe that she had been hoping to find out that information from them.

For several minutes she said nothing, alternately staring at the fireplace and the two boys.

All of a sudden she rose from her chair. "It just occurred to me that I was supposed to call a friend of mine about dinner tomorrow," she said. "Please excuse me. I shan't be long." With that Senhora de Feira left the room.

"What do you think?" Joe whispered to Frank.

"I don't feel good about any of this," Frank replied.

"Me neither," Joe said. "But what are we going to do?"

Frank shrugged. "Did you notice when I mentioned the problems that Frau Rilke's family is having, Senhora de Feira didn't even respond?" he asked. "All she seemed concerned about was the gold."

Joe nodded. "She said she could remember the story very well," he said, "but I think she remembers it because it's been on her mind all these years."

"I think you're right, and that bothers me," Frank agreed. "She almost seemed, well, *greedy* about it."

"We did learn one thing," Joe said. "Senhora

de Feira doesn't know that the gold is buried in the backyard across the street. She really does think it's buried in one of Lisbon's parks. Do you think we should tell her that it's not?"

Frank thought for a minute. "If we put ourselves in her place, maybe we'd want some of the gold too." He looked around. "At first I thought this place was really elegant, but now I think it's probably seen better days. It's beginning to look kind of shabby."

"That could be the reason why it's so dark in here," Joe said. "Maybe Senhora de Feira is ashamed of how the house looks."

"That has to be it, Joe—that's why she's so interested in the gold. Her family probably needs money too," Frank said. "But what choice do we have? We can't just go back across the street and start digging in Senhora Bragança's backyard. We could show Senhora de Feira the map and ask her advice on how we could . . ."

Before he could finish his sentence, however, Senhora de Feira returned to the room. "I'm glad that's taken care of," she said, sitting back down in her chair. "I'm getting so forgetful these days. Now where were we?"

"You were a very special friend of Frau Rilke's," Joe said. "She trusted you so much that she told you about the gold—so we thought that perhaps you could help us find it and, once we recover it, get it back to the United States."

Senhora de Feira laughed. "You must not have been listening when I was talking to you earlier," she said. "We have no way of knowing in which park the gold is buried."

"Actually, Frau Rilke gave us a map that shows the location," Joe said.

Senhora de Feira gasped and clutched at her throat. "Oh, please let me see it!" she managed to say.

Just as Joe started to reach inside his coat pocket three young men came into the room. They were dressed much like the men whom Frank and Joe had seen earlier on their way into Lisbon—the men whom Inspector Oliveira had referred to as fascists. One was holding a leash with a snarling Doberman at the end of it.

Startled, the Hardy boys jumped up from the sofa.

"What's going on here?" Frank asked.

"My sons," Senhora de Feira announced. "Paulo, Antonio, and Rafael."

The three men nodded at the Hardy boys and walked into the room.

"This is Frank and Joe Hardy from America," Senhora de Feira said. "They're friends of Brigette Fleissner, and they've come here to take her suitcase of gold bars back with them."

At that, Senhora de Feira's sons grinned.

"How do they propose to do that?" Paulo asked.

For a moment the room was quiet. Suddenly Senhora de Feira looked curiously at Frank and Joe. "Boys, Paulo asked you a question. Why are you so nervous?"

"It's the uniforms," Frank said. "Our father's friend, Inspector Oliveira of the Lisbon Police Department, said that only members of fascist groups wear them."

Paulo, Antonio, and Rafael laughed.

"We're in a play about a fascist group," Antonio said. "That's why we're dressed this way."

"Yes, that's why," Rafael agreed.

Frank could tell that they were lying, but he also knew that if he and Joe planned to get out of there alive, he couldn't let the sons know what he was thinking. "Oh. Well, I wish you a lot of success with the play," he said. "Maybe we'll try to see it before we go back home."

"Right," Joe said. "Maybe you could tell us where we can get tickets?"

"Oh, don't worry about that. We'll get tickets for you," Paulo said. "But we'd like to hear more about Brigette Fleissner. Mother has really missed her."

Senhora de Feira nodded. "You said she gave you a map of where the suitcase is buried," she said. "Would you please show it to us?"

Joe withdrew his hand from his pocket. "I can't believe this—I must have left it at the hotel!" he said. "I guess Frank and I will just have to go back there and get it."

"Perhaps you should look in one of your other pockets," Antonio suggested. "Maybe you forgot where you put it."

Frank glanced quickly around the room. He and Joe were trapped.

5 Intruder in the Dark

Joe looked over at Frank. "Ets-lay am-scray!" he said.

Frank grinned. *Pig Latin,* he thought. *Perfect!* "Ood-gay an-play, other-bray!" he said to Joe.

"What are you saying?" Antonio demanded. "Speak English!"

"Or Portuguese!" Paulo added. "We don't know that language!"

"Oo-tay ad-bay!" Joe said. He leaned forward on the sofa, as if preparing to run a race. "Ow-nay!"

Frank got the message. He shot off the sofa a split second behind Joe.

Before Senhora de Feira and her sons realized what was happening, Frank and Joe were almost to the front door of the de Feira house.

Behind them they heard the de Feiras shouting and the Doberman barking.

Joe reached the door first. He turned the large iron knob to open the door.

Frank, right behind him, ran out and shut it behind him, just as the Doberman reached it. The dog squealed in pain as it crashed into the thick wood.

Frank and Joe raced down the porch steps and out to the street.

"I hope there's a crowd of people at the tram station," Joe shouted to Frank. "Safety in numbers!"

Frank knew he was right. He didn't think the de Feira brothers would threaten them if there were other people around.

When they were two blocks away from the de Feira house, Joe looked over his shoulder. He was surprised to see that nobody was coming after them. Cautiously he slowed down.

Frank, noticing that Joe had decreased his pace, turned and looked behind them. "I wonder where they are," he said.

Now the two of them were jogging at a more leisurely pace.

"I don't know," Joe said. "They might be follow-ing us on a parallel street."

"Or they might not be following us at all," Frank said. Now he was just walking fast.

"Do you think we overreacted a bit?" Joe asked.

Frank shrugged. "They seemed pretty spooky to me," he said. "I didn't believe that story about being in a play for one minute."

"Me neither," Joe said. "They must belong to one of those fascist organizations that Inspector Oliveira was talking about."

"Of course, that doesn't necessarily mean they'd do something to us, Joe," Frank said. "They might save their fights for their fellow citizens."

They walked the rest of the way to the tram station. The tram that would take them from Belém to Lisbon proper was arriving just as they got there.

Once back at the hotel, Frank and Joe headed up to their room, which was across the hall from their parents' room. Joe telephoned them to let them know they were back.

"You're just in time for dinner," Mr. Hardy said. "We'll meet you two in the lobby in ten minutes. Tonight we're going to eat in the hotel."

"Sounds good," Joe said.

Joe reached inside his jacket pocket and pulled out the map that Frau Rilke had drawn for them. "We should put this in the hotel's safe," he said. "I don't want to chance losing it."

"Yeah—good idea," Frank agreed. "For a minute there, I thought one of the de Feira brothers might tackle us and try to steal the map."

41

Frank and Joe took turns washing up and then headed down to the hotel lobby.

Joe handed the map to one of the desk clerks. "This is an important document," he said. "I'd like to put it in the hotel safe, please."

"Yes, sir," the clerk said. He put the map inside a brown envelope and wrote their room number on it. "It will be very safe, sir," he added with a smile.

"Thank you," Joe said.

He and Frank strolled around the lobby and looked in the shops while they waited for their parents.

One shop in particular had some cool-looking Portuguese shoes, which they thought Callie and Iola would like.

"We should get something for Catarina, too," Joe said. "I wonder what she'd like."

Frank shrugged. "I'm sure we'll find something."

Just then Mr. and Mrs. Hardy and Aunt Gertrude stepped off the elevator and walked toward Frank and Joe.

"There are three restaurants in this hotel," Mr. Hardy said. "Your mother and Aunt Gertrude want to eat at Picanha."

"We're game for anything," Frank said.

"Well," Aunt Gertrude said, "they only serve *picanha*."

Frank and Joe looked at each other.

"Okay, I give up," Joe said. "What is *picanha*?"

"It's a special Portuguese dish," Mrs. Hardy said. "Rump steak served with salad, rice, and beans."

"Well, that sounds good. I could really eat anything," Joe said. "Let's go for it."

When they got to the restaurant, their waiter took them right to a table. Since *picanha* was the only dish the restaurant served, they didn't need to order, and in a short time their meal arrived.

"Great choice!" Frank exclaimed after a few bites. "Delicious."

Everyone agreed.

Although Mr. and Mrs. Hardy were used to Frank and Joe's involvement in dangerous projects, Frank and Joe had decided on the way back to the hotel to not volunteer any specific information about what had happened. They didn't want their parents to be too alarmed.

When Mr. Hardy asked about their trip to Belém, Frank skirted the episode at the de Feira residence. "We didn't accomplish much. We've got to think up a new tack, but we've got some ideas."

Mr. Hardy nodded. "Oh, by the way," he said, "we're all expected at the Oliveiras' house at ten."

"Why so late?" Aunt Gertrude asked.

"Europeans just start the evening later than Americans," Mr. Hardy explained.

Joe said, "Tell us what you know about Lisbon during the Second World War, Dad."

"Well, I don't know anything firsthand," Mr. Hardy said with a laugh, "but I've talked to a few men and women who were here at the time, and I've read a lot."

"I've seen a lot of spy movies that were set in Lisbon," Aunt Gertrude volunteered. "There was a lot of anger here at one time, I think."

For the next few minutes Mr. Hardy told his sons about all the intrigues in Lisbon that had occurred during World War II because Portugal had remained neutral. "That meant everyone could fight the war without actually fighting the war," he said. "Of course, ostensibly the Portuguese could expel you if you did something that they thought violated their neutrality, but in reality a lot of spying went on, and a lot of people were taken out of the country against their will."

After wartime Lisbon had been exhausted as a conversation topic, Mr. and Mrs. Hardy talked about their afternoon.

"I tried sitting in that little park across the street," Aunt Gertrude said, "but these men kept flirting with me. I just got disgusted and came back to the hotel."

Joe kicked Frank under the table. They both knew that even though Aunt Gertrude complained about the attention she had gotten in the park, she was probably very happy about it. In fact, they were sure of it when Aunt Gertrude added, "If that happens again tomorrow, when I go back over there to get some sun, then I'm really going to be irritated."

Frank and Joe could barely keep themselves from laughing!

When the meal was over, Mr. and Mrs. Hardy and Aunt Gertrude suggested they take a stroll down the broad Avenida da Liberdade, which was just a half block over from the hotel.

"I want to do some people-watching," Mrs. Hardy said. "It's the best way to get a feel for a city."

"It'll be a while before we go over to the Oliveiras' house," Mr. Hardy said. "Do you boys want to come along?"

Frank and Joe declined the invitation. "We need to think about how we're going to help our friend Frau Rilke, Dad," Joe said, "so we'll just go on back to our room."

"Okay, boys," Mr. Hardy said. "We'll check in with you when we get back."

Frank and Joe left their parents and Aunt Gertrude at the restaurant's entrance and headed toward the bank of elevators that would take them back up to their room.

"That really was a great meal," Joe said, "but I think I ate too much."

"Maybe we should have walked it off after all," Frank said. "It's probably not too late to catch them. I don't think they're walking all that fast."

Joe shook his head. "I'd rather watch some television and try to figure out our next move," he said. "Frankly, I've done enough people-watching today!"

Frank laughed. "I guess you're right," he said as he inserted the key into the door. "Hey," he said, opening the door, "didn't we turn off the lights?"

"Yeah," Joe said as they entered the room. "I'm sure we . . ."

Just then something hit Joe's head, knocking him against a wall and causing him to momentarily see stars. "Ow!" he cried, grabbing his head with his hands.

Across the room Frank saw a man dressed in black head for an open window. "Hey!" he cried. "Stop!" Behind him Joe was still groaning. Feeling he should take care of his brother before anything else, Frank turned and hurried to his side.

Joe, shaking off the effects of the attack, quickly assured Frank he was okay. "Let's get him!" he said, regaining his balance.

By the time Frank turned back around, though, the man had disappeared.

The teens rushed to the window and looked out.

They immediately spotted the man. He was fleeing down the fire escape.

"We've done this before," Joe shouted. "Let's go after him!"

Joe climbed through the window first, glad to feel the cool night air on his throbbing head, and started after the man.

Behind him Frank slipped, but he grabbed the rail just in time.

The man was halfway down the building's side now. The only light helping the Hardys to see came from the hotel's windows. It wasn't enough light for them to be able to identify the intruder, but Joe had a pretty good idea of who he was.

By now the man had reached the bottom landing, which was still several feet above the ground. He looked up once, but his face was still so obscured by the darkness that it was impossible to make out any features. He quickly jumped to the alley below and sprinted away.

"We can't let him get away!" Joe shouted. Now he had reached the bottom landing himself, and without any hesitation he jumped several feet to the alley below.

Frank was sure that Joe's head had probably suffered additional shock from the impact of jumping, but he was impressed that it hadn't kept Joe from running after the intruder at full speed.

Frank reached the bottom landing a split second after his brother, jumped down to the alley, and followed Joe.

The alley was long and lit with spotlights from the backs of the buildings it bordered. Overflowing garbage cans narrowed the alley.

Up ahead, the fugitive deliberately tipped over garbage cans to slow down the Hardys. For the next several minutes Frank and Joe had to tromp through foul-smelling garbage to catch up with the man.

Finally Frank and Joe reached the end of the garbage-filled alley, but the man jumped into a waiting car and sped away.

"You know who that was, don't you?" Frank said.

"Well, I don't know *exactly* which one of Senhora de Feira's sons it was," Joe said, "but I do know that it was one of them."

"That was a brilliant idea you had, Joe—to put Frau Rilke's map in the hotel safe," Frank said. "I'm sure that's what the guy was after."

"Now what?" Joe said.

Frank sniffed his shirt and grimaced. "Well, the first thing we need to do is take showers."

"Yeah. We'll probably need to go back the way we came," Joe added, "because smelling like this, we probably won't be allowed through the front door of the hotel."

"You're probably right," Frank said.

They headed back down the alley, trying to avoid as much of the spilled garbage as possible. "We know one thing now," Joe said. "This mission isn't going to be as easy as we'd hoped."

6 A Real-life Movie

Frank and Joe hurried back up the fire escape to the open window of their room and climbed through.

"Whichever de Feira brother that was, he must have broken the lock on the window and come into our room that way," Joe said, examining the metal hooks. But when he found that nothing appeared broken and that the window locked when he turned the mechanism, he added, "Wait—scratch that. The lock works perfectly."

"That means he got in through the door," Frank said. "He either managed to get a pass key or he knows how to use burglar's tools."

Joe opened the door to their room and examined

its locking mechanism. Not seeing any scratch marks, he closed the door and said, "I vote for a pass key, Frank. Dad told us that these guys have all kinds of connections."

"That's scary. This means we're not really safe in our room," Frank said. "I think we need to tell Dad and then notify the hotel authorities."

"But if we tell Dad, he and Mom will make us move into their room," Joe said.

"Right," Frank agreed. "Hmm . . . I don't like the thought of that."

"Not only *that*," Joe continued, "but we don't want to scare off the de Feira brothers. We want to catch them in the act. Right?"

Just then there was a knock at the door. "We're back from our walk, boys," Mr. Hardy said. "Are you ready to go to Inspector Oliveira's house?"

"Just give us a few minutes, Dad!" Joe called through the door. "We need to finish cleaning up."

"Okay," Mr. Hardy said. "Five minutes."

Frank and Joe ran around their room, shedding their dirty clothes and pulling clean clothes out of the armoires. Joe took a quick shower. When Joe jumped out, Frank jumped in.

They had just finished combing their hair when Mr. Hardy knocked on their door again. "Come on, boys. We need to leave."

Joe opened the door. "No problem, Dad," he

said. He grinned at Frank. "In fact, we were wondering what was keeping you."

Mr. Hardy sniffed the room. "Something stinks in there," he said.

"We were thinking the same thing, Dad," Frank said, closing the door behind him and Joe. "I'll report it to the manager tomorrow."

Inspector Oliveira had sent a police department van to take the Hardys to his house. The driver didn't mind using the sirens and the blue dome light to speed them through the evening traffic in the heart of the city.

Inspector Oliveira and his family lived across the Tagus River, which was spanned by the enormous Ponte 25 de Abril in the Lisbon suburb of Cacilhas on the Setúbal peninsula. When they reached the center of the bridge, the driver pulled over into a police lane and stopped so that the Hardys could take in the view.

"Oh, it's so gorgeous," Aunt Gertrude said. "Lisbon is such a beautiful city."

"*Muito obrigada, Senhora,*" the driver said. "Thank you very much."

Once they were back in traffic the driver informed them that they were only ten minutes from Inspector Oliveira's house. Joe took this as a challenge. So he checked his watch and was impressed that the driver was right on target—almost to the second.

"Goodness! There's a crowd of people here,"

Mrs. Hardy said. "I thought it was just going to be a small reception."

"Oh no, miss," the driver said. "Most of the police officers in Lisbon are here tonight to meet the famous Fenton Hardy from the United States."

Frank knew that his father was probably groaning inside. He much preferred smaller gatherings and discussing details of the various mysteries that were stumping detectives all over the world. Mr. Hardy was usually able to offer some suggestions to help solve these cases.

"There's Inspector Oliveira now," the driver said. He nodded toward the front door of the house. "He must have been watching for us."

"Great," Mr. Hardy said.

Just as Inspector Oliveira reached the van a voice called from the porch of the house. "Father? Is that the Hardys?"

"Yes, Isabel!" Inspector Oliveira called back. "Come and meet everyone."

Joe gave the inspector a puzzled look. No one had mentioned that he had a daughter. "This night could turn out to be more interesting than we thought," he whispered to Frank.

As Frank watched the girl approach, he said, "I think you're right!"

When Isabel reached the group, Inspector Oliveira introduced her to everyone.

"Oh, Isabel, you are absolutely lovely," Aunt

Gertrude said. "You look like a movie star."

Isabel smiled. "Well, actually, I have been an extra in a couple of Portuguese movies. Nothing really big, but it was fun. I'm hoping that one day, well . . . let's just say a trip to Hollywood is a dream of mine!"

"Wow!" Frank and Joe said in unison, causing everyone to laugh.

"Isabel, even though Frank and Joe are well-known for solving mysteries, I think they'd have more fun with you than with us old folks," Inspector Oliveira said. "Why don't you take over from here? Okay, guys?"

"That sounds good to me," Joe said.

"Ditto," Frank agreed.

As the three teens headed back to the house together Frank turned to Isabel. "Your father sometimes talks like an American. Where did he learn his English?"

"Texas," Isabel replied.

"*Texas?*" Frank said. "You're kidding."

Isabel smiled. "No, I'm serious. He got his master's degree in forensic science at Texas Tech University in Lubbock about five years ago. I spent a year at one of the high schools there."

When they reached the front porch, Frank noticed two entrances. Isabel opened the door on the left. "Welcome to my house, gentlemen!" she said.

"Wow. This is a great place!" Frank said, looking around.

"I wouldn't mind having a pad like this myself back in Bayport," Joe echoed.

"Have a seat and I'll get us some *Sumol*," Isabel said. "It's a good thing to drink in Portugal. It's really fizzy and comes in all kinds of fruit flavors."

"Sounds good," Frank and Joe said.

Within a couple of minutes, Isabel returned with a tray and three drinks. She handed one each to Frank and Joe, took the third one, and then sat down in a plush chair opposite the boys.

"After Mother died three years ago, Father redid the entire house," Isabel explained. "He said he wanted to give me privacy." She smiled. "While that was true, I also think he was hoping that if I felt I had my own apartment, I'd want to stay here—at least for a few years, until he got used to being without my mother."

"It must have worked," Frank said.

Isabel nodded. "I wouldn't have left anyway because my father has always respected my privacy. After Mother died, though, I just wanted to stay near him to make sure he was all right."

"He seems all right to me," Joe said.

"For the most part he is because he keeps very busy—but I still worry about him sometimes," Isabel said. "He was really looking forward to your visit. He has such respect for your father."

"I think the feeling is mutual, Isabel," Frank said.

"Your parents seem to feel the same way about

you guys, too," Isabel said. "I'd say we're among the lucky few in this world."

Frank and Joe nodded.

"Well, tell me about Frank and Joe Hardy, boy detectives," Isabel said. "Naturally, having a policeman for a father, all of my life I've been around issues that require police involvement. Sometimes I even think about giving up on trying to become a movie star and instead going for a degree in criminal justice. I love adventure!"

Frank and Joe took turns telling Isabel about some of the mysteries they had solved, not only in Bayport but all over the world.

"In fact," Joe said, "we're working on solving a mystery here in Lisbon."

Isabel's eyes widened. "Really? What is it?"

Joe glanced at his brother to see if Frank agreed with his decision to share Frau Rilke's secret with Isabel. He got an almost imperceptible nod. Joe was sure that Frank felt the same way he felt: that Isabel Oliveira would be a tremendous asset and a great ally in helping them to recover Frau Rilke's suitcase of gold bars.

When the Hardy boys finished telling Frau Rilke's story, Isabel seemed stunned by what she had just heard.

"It's like a movie plot," she finally said, then blushed. "Oh, I'm sorry. I know Frau Rilke's family went through terrible times during that war, and I shouldn't . . ."

"Oh no, Isabel, you're right—it really *is* just like a movie," Frank said, "but in this case, this is reality and this woman needs our help."

Isabel stood up. "More *Sumol*?" she said.

"Please!" Joe said.

"It's really good," Frank said. "I wish we could get this in Bayport."

"Well, I know it's exported to the U.S.," Isabel said, "but it may not be available everywhere."

"We'll ask our Portuguese friend Catarina about it when we get back to Bayport," Joe said. "If she doesn't know, then I'm sure someone in her family would."

When Isabel came back with refilled glasses, she said, "Unfortunately there are a lot of young fascists in this country now and people are starting to take them more seriously. I think we need to be very careful."

"After our visit to Senhora de Feira's house and the encounter with her sons, I'd agree," Joe said.

"Isabel, we're fairly certain that the man who broke into our room at the hotel is one of the de Feira brothers," Frank added, "so we know they're serious."

"I don't even think we should tell my father about it yet," Isabel said.

That comment surprised the Hardy boys.

"Why?" Frank asked.

"My father is a very good policeman," Isabel explained, "but sometimes he's blind to the indiscretions of men and women on his side."

"What are you saying?" Joe asked. "That there are Lisbon police officers who are fascists?"

Isabel nodded. "I've heard things about some of them," she said. "Of course, there's nothing that anyone can prove. They're too smart for that. Anyway, it's probably best if we keep this to ourselves for a while."

"Okay, if you think so," Joe said.

"I'm curious if there's any talk on the streets about that suitcase with the gold bars," Isabel said. "I can ask around a bit."

"Do you think the de Feiras would really go around talking about it?" Frank asked. "Wouldn't they want to keep it quiet, so they wouldn't have any competition?"

"That's what I'd do," Joe said.

"They might just brag about it without giving away too much information," Frank said.

"It's possible," Isabel said. She hesitated for a minute. "What we don't want is for word to get around Lisbon that a map exists, showing the exact location of that suitcase," she continued. "If that happens, your lives could be in serious danger."

"Well, after the incident tonight at the hotel I'd say that is a definite possibility," Joe said.

"I agree with Joe, Isabel," Frank added. "Those de Feira brothers seem dangerous."

"It's not the de Feira brothers I'm worried about. My father says they're not really violent. They just try to intimidate," Isabel said. "I'm worried about men who wouldn't think twice about dumping your bodies off the Ponte 25 de Abril!"

7 The Fake Maps

Frank and Joe were still in bed the next morning when the telephone rang.

Frank picked up the receiver. "Hello," he said sleepily.

"Frank! It's Isabel Oliveira," Isabel said. "We've got problems."

Instantly Frank was wide awake. "Joe," he whispered. "It's Isabel!"

Joe sat up slowly, trying to come back from the dream he was having about him and Frank solving a sensational crime back in Bayport. "What's wrong?"

"What happened, Isabel?" Frank said into the receiver. "Are you all right?"

"It's about Frau Rilke's suitcase," Isabel said.

"What about it?" Frank said.

Joe was now out of bed and sitting beside Frank, his ear as close to the receiver as possible.

"I overheard some of Father's men talking on the police radio this morning," Isabel explained. "Evidently the word on the streets is—and I quote—you and Joe have a map that shows where some gold bars are buried here in Lisbon."

"Great," Frank said. "Now what?"

"I don't think that anyone except us knows that the gold is in the backyard of Senhora Bragança's house," Isabel said. "So for right now it should be safe. But I'm worried about you two."

"So am I," Frank said.

Joe leaned away from the receiver and nodded. "You got that right," he said.

"I have to be at the television studio in a few minutes, so I need to leave," Isabel said, "but I just wanted to warn you to be careful."

"Thanks, Isabel," Frank said. "We'll talk to you later."

"Something doesn't make sense here, Frank," Joe said. "Last night Isabel seemed certain that the de Feira brothers wouldn't spread the word around Lisbon about the map. What happened?"

"They're just dumb," Frank said.

"Do you really think they're *that* dumb, Frank?" Joe asked.

For several minutes Frank didn't say anything. Finally he looked at Joe with an expression of both anger and disappointment. "Well, there is only one other way that it could have happened, Joe, and I don't like what it means."

Joe nodded slowly. "Do you think Isabel is behind it?" he asked.

"A good detective would have to consider that as a possibility, Joe," Frank said.

"But her father is a high-ranking police official," Joe protested.

Frank shrugged. "This sort of thing has happened before," he reminded Joe.

"It's hard to trust anyone these days," Joe said sadly.

"I know," Frank said. He stood up and stretched. "For now it's just speculation on my part, though, and there really could be another explanation."

"I hope so," Joe said. "I really like Isabel."

"I do too," Frank said. "We just need to do what we always do, Joe, and that's to keep an open mind."

"I wonder now if that intruder last night was really one of the de Feira brothers," Joe said.

"I was thinking that too," Frank said.

"Well, we've got to do something about this," Joe said. "Maybe we could come up with a plan to send everyone on a wild goose chase."

They debated about different ways to do that, but none of their ideas seemed feasible.

Finally Joe said, "I know! A fake map!"

Frank looked at him. "What do you mean, a fake map?"

"Well, Isabel is the only one who knows that the real map is of Senhora Bragança's backyard—but she doesn't know *exactly* where the suitcase is buried," Joe explained.

"Right," Frank said. "That would keep her—and whomever else she might have told—from getting the suitcase because they couldn't just go in and dig up the entire backyard."

Joe nodded. "If they knew the exact spot, then they'd have no problem finding the gold if it's still there."

"So this new map would put the suitcase in an area as far away from the real location as possible?" Frank said.

For a minute Joe didn't say anything. Then he jumped off the bed and started pacing around the room. Finally he shouted, "Wait—we need *two* maps!"

"Two maps?" Frank said. "Why?"

Joe returned to his bed and sat down. "Well, we'll make a new map of Senhora Bragança's backyard as a safety—just in case Isabel isn't really our friend—and we'll hope in the meantime that she is," Joe said. "The other map will place the gold in an entirely different location, and this will be for the de Feiras and anybody else who Isabel believes is involved."

Frank thought for a minute. "Complicated but

63

necessary," he said, "and I think this just might work."

Frank and Joe dressed quickly and took the elevator down to the lobby. They asked the clerk at the front desk for the envelope that they had put in the safe the day before.

After they got the map the teens went back up to their room and redrew the map of Senhora Bragança's backyard. This time they put the X as far away from the real location of the suitcase as possible.

Joe put the fake map in his pocket, then he and Frank went back downstairs and returned the brown envelope containing the real map to the desk clerk.

As they headed back up to their room for a second time, Joe said, "We need to study a map of Lisbon and find a big park that has a lot of secluded areas where someone could have buried a suitcase full of gold bars."

Frank nodded. "That Lisbon guidebook in our room will give us the information we need," he said, "and it'll also let us know if the park existed in 1943."

"Oh yeah—I forgot about that!" Joe said. "Couldn't have put the gold in a park that wasn't around then."

Back in their room Frank got out the guidebook to Lisbon. For several minutes they studied the different maps that showed park locations all over the city.

"Maybe we should choose one that's not too far from where Frau Rilke's family lived. If her father had walked all over Lisbon carrying a suitcase, he would have attracted a lot of unwanted attention," Joe said.

"Well, Joe, remember that Dad said there were a lot of refugees in Lisbon then, so a suitcase in itself might not have been a problem," Frank countered. "A suitcase full of gold bars would have been heavy, though, and it would have been difficult for Herr Fleissner to carry it too far. That's probably the best reason for him going to a park that was nearby."

"Oh yeah, that's right," Joe agreed.

They decided to concentrate their efforts in Belém, where the Fleissners had lived.

"Here's a park that was built in the early 1900s to showcase the plants and trees from the Portuguese colonies all over the world," Joe said. "The Jardim Agrícola Tropical. And the location is just about right."

Frank read the description of the park. "Perfect!" he said. "This is now the location of Frau Rilke's suitcase full of gold bars."

Frank and Joe drew the new map and put an X in a secluded part of the park, near some dragon trees from the Madeira Islands.

"We'll leave this map lying around the room and then when someone—," Frank started to say.

But Joe interrupted. "Wait—I just thought of a better idea!"

"Okay, what is it?" Frank said.

"We'll go to the Jardim Agrícola Tropical ourselves and dig up the suitcase!" Joe exclaimed.

Frank looked at him for a couple of seconds, then said, "But Joe, hello—this map's fake."

"I know it's a fake, Frank," Joe said, rolling his eyes. "But what we're going to do is buy one of those little fold-up shovels so we can hide it easily—and take it to the park along with this map. And we'll see what happens."

Frank's eyes widened and a big grin spread over his face. "So you think that somebody will follow us to the fake location?"

"That's what I'm hoping!" Joe said. "If they do, they'll probably wait until we're just about ready to start digging and then will surprise us. Of course we'll drop everything—the shovel, the map, *everything*—and run from the park as if we're scared to death."

"Then whoever followed us will start digging up the whole Jardim Agrícola Tropical, hoping to find the suitcase," Frank said. "Brilliant!" He paused. "Except I'd hate to have that beautiful park destroyed."

"Oh, I don't think they'll really get too far before the authorities stop them," Joe said. "Remember that we'll have our shovel hidden, and we've put the

X in a really secluded part of the park, so I don't think the authorities will bother us—but when whoever follows us can't find the suitcase in the spot we've marked on the map, they'll probably start digging all around the area. That's when the park authorities will stop them."

Frank laughed. "They'll be so frustrated! They'll probably spend *weeks* trying to outsmart the park police in order to get a suitcase that isn't there."

"That's what I hope will happen," Joe said. "In the meantime we'll try to figure out a way to dig up the real suitcase at Senhora Bragança's house."

"I just thought of something else, Joe," Frank said. "We'll also solve another problem."

"What?" Joe asked.

"If we really are followed to the Jardim Agrícola Tropical, then we'll know that Isabel was telling the truth," Frank said. "She knows that the suitcase is buried in Senhora Bragança's backyard. I don't think she—or anyone she might have told—would follow us to this other park."

"Right," Joe said. "I really do hope Isabel's innocent."

After checking in with Mr. Hardy and telling him that they were still working on Frau Rilke's case, Frank and Joe took the elevator down to the lobby. A man at the concierge's desk told them that there was a camping-supply store just two blocks from the hotel. He said that they should be able to buy a fold-up shovel there, and he asked if they needed the locations of some nearby campsites.

"No," Joe responded. "We already know where we're going."

"But thanks anyway," Frank added.

The Hardy boys found the camping-supply store without any trouble, bought the fold-up shovel and a small canvas bag for carrying it, and then they headed to the tram to Belém.

As they were boarding the train Joe whispered, "Have you noticed anyone suspicious?"

Frank shook his head. "No, but I'm trying to act as normal as possible and not seem too suspicious myself. I don't want anybody to think that we know they're following us."

The tram wasn't overly crowded when it left downtown Lisbon, but the closer it got to Belém, the more crowded it became. Soon it was hard to see past the people who were standing right around them.

Finally a recorded voice announced in Portuguese and English that the next stop was the Jardim Agrícola Tropical.

Frank and Joe stood up and slowly moved through the crowd of passengers to the rear door of the tram.

Once Frank thought he noticed a man watching them with more than just passing interest, but when he looked at the man again, he was reading a newspaper.

When the doors opened, Frank and Joe jumped off. They knew that several other passengers got off too, but they purposely didn't turn around to look, just in case it might scare off whoever might be following them to the park.

The teens found the entrance to the park, paid the small entrance fee, and then, after consulting a park map, headed for the area where they had marked the phony X—near the dragon trees.

Frank had read that for some reason this park didn't attract many visitors, so it was perfect for their mission.

"This is it, I think," Joe said. He was looking at a sign in Portuguese. "I recognize the word for dragon."

Frank stopped, bent down, and started retying his shoelace. At the same time he noticed that no one was behind them. *Of course,* he thought, *if somebody is following us, they would try not to be too obvious about it. At this very moment they could be observing us from behind some of the trees.*

"See anything?" Joe whispered when Frank had straightened up.

"No," Frank whispered back. He knew that Joe had used the same maneuver while on other cases.

"Okay, we're here. Let's just hope that the suitcase is still here too," Joe said, talking not so loud that it seemed unnatural but not so quietly that anyone nearby wouldn't have heard him. He took the map out of his pocket and pointed to it. "The spot where we need to start digging should be around those trees over there." He pretended to look at one particular tree. "Come on, Frank!"

Frank, taking the hint, took the fold-up shovel out of the canvas bag and unfolded it.

As the Hardys entered the area of the dragon trees Frank thought he heard a noise to his left—but he willed himself not to look in that direction.

Joe must have heard it too, because he said, "It's been a long time coming, but in a minute we're going to be really rich!" This time he spoke loud enough for anyone to hear.

At that moment a loud crashing noise made Frank and Joe turn to their left. Two men were rushing toward them.

Frank dropped the shovel and the canvas bag and Joe dropped the map—just as they had planned to do—and they ran as fast as they could toward the main park entrance.

No one followed them.

When they reached the entrance, they nodded to the park official and then left the park, heading back to the tram stop.

"Looks like it worked," Joe said.

"Good plan, Joe," Frank told him. "We know now that Isabel is okay to trust."

"What's next?" Joe asked.

"We have to figure out a way to convince Senhora Bragança to let us dig up her backyard," Frank said.

"That means buying another fold-up shovel and canvas bag from the camping-supply store," Joe said.

"If this little ruse keeps people from bothering us, it'll be worth it," Frank said.

8 Dog Attack!

Frank and Joe waited anxiously for all the passengers to board the tram that would take them back to central Lisbon. Finally the doors closed and the tram started.

"I don't think anybody followed us," Frank said. "The other people onboard are mostly women and elderly men."

Joe nodded. "Those men are too busy digging up the Jardim Agrícola Tropical," he said. "I wonder how long it'll be before they realize the map was a fake."

"It may be a while, Joe," Frank said. "I think we gave a pretty good performance back there."

Joe grinned. "Yeah," he said. "I think the way I

dropped that map and ran away should earn me an acting award!"

"Well, you should have seen the way I dropped the shovel and the canvas bag," Frank said. "Talk about great acting!"

"Let's not rest on our acting laurels just yet, though," Joe said. "We need to get the *real* suitcase as soon as possible."

"Right," Frank agreed. "We can only keep those guys fooled for so long."

"What about going after the gold tonight?" Joe said.

"I think that's a good idea," Frank said. "But we'll have to figure out a way to get into the backyard—past the guards and the dogs."

"We've overcome greater odds before," Joe said. "Between now and tonight, I'm sure we'll figure out something."

For the rest of the trip Frank and Joe enjoyed the scenery. On the walk back to the hotel they decided to buy another shovel and canvas bag at the camping-supply store.

The same clerk waited on them. "If there's something wrong with what you bought earlier, you may return it," he said.

"Oh no, we just need another set," Frank said.

"We're letting somebody else use what we bought this morning," Joe said.

That story seemed to satisfy the clerk. He wrapped up the new shovel and canvas bag. At the last minute Joe added a small flashlight and paid for it with some Portuguese money.

"We need to call Isabel and tell her what happened," Frank said as they left the camping-supply store.

"Right," Joe said. "It was silly to think she was somehow involved with those fascist groups."

When Frank and Joe got back to their hotel, they called their parents to let them know that they were all right.

Mrs. Hardy asked them if they'd like to go to a movie that evening. "The concierge told us that there's a theater just a couple of blocks away that plays American movies," she said. "Aunt Gertrude would like to hear some English—she's already feeling a little homesick!"

"We're going to call Isabel to see if she wants to do something tonight," Frank told their mother. "Thanks for the invitation, though."

"All right . . . but if you change your mind, the movie starts at eight o'clock," Mrs. Hardy said.

"Thanks, Mom," Frank said.

After Frank hung up Joe dialed Isabel's number. She answered on the third ring. He told her what had taken place at the Jardim Agrícola Tropical.

"Oh, that was such a brilliant plan!" Isabel said.

"No wonder Frank and Joe Hardy are known far and wide for solving mysteries."

"We have another brilliant plan," Joe told her. "And we hope you'll want to be part of it."

"I trust you guys so much that I'll say yes before you even tell me what it is," Isabel said.

"Now, that's what I call having faith in someone!" Joe said.

Isabel laughed.

Joe told her their plan to find a way into Senhora Bragança's backyard that night and to dig up the suitcase.

For a few seconds Isabel didn't say anything, and Joe wondered if she was having second thoughts about going with them. But then she said, "It's not stealing because the gold belongs to Frau Rilke—and I'm sure we can talk our way out of any trespassing complaint."

"That's what we were thinking," Joe said.

"The Portuguese courts would surely give us permission to dig, anyway—but then, getting that approval would probably take months and months, and I know that you don't have that much time," Isabel added.

"No, we don't—and neither does Frau Rilke," Joe said.

"We're probably stretching the law here, but those were terrible times," Isabel said, "and I know the Portuguese people would be on our side."

"Well, maybe not *everybody*," Joe said. "Those fascists would probably figure out a way to get that money instead of Frau Rilke."

"Which, as far as I'm concerned, is a very strong argument for going to Senhora Bragança's house tonight," Isabel said.

"Can you pick us up at the hotel in your car?" Joe said.

"No problem," Isabel said. "What time?"

Joe looked over at Frank. "What time should Isabel come by?" he asked.

"Ten o'clock," Frank said. "We need to be there by eleven."

Joe repeated the information to Isabel.

"Okay—I'll be waiting for you in front of the hotel at ten," Isabel said. "Look for a red Porsche."

"We'll be there," Joe told her.

When Joe hung up the receiver, he said, "Why ten? We never really talked about that. Do you know something that I don't?"

"I just remembered that when we were at Senhora Bragança's house the first time, the car with the domestic help arrived just before 3 P.M.," Frank said. "That's the beginning of a normal work shift."

"Oh, yeah!" Joe said. "7 A.M. to 3 P.M., 3 P.M. to 11 P.M., and 11 P.M. to 7 A.M."

"Exactly. So if we're there when the car brings in the domestic help at around 11 P.M., we can follow the car through the gate," Frank said. "I think that's the only way we can get past the security guards."

"What about the dogs?" Joe said. "Once we're inside, won't they pick up our scents?"

"We'll bring a little fresh meat and a mild sedative. Nothing that will harm them," Frank said. "We'll get some kind of ground meat and an over-the-counter sleep aid."

Another conversation with the concierge led Frank and Joe to a nearby meat market, where they bought a pound of ground pork. After that they went two doors down to a pharmacy where—after pondering which one of the many sleep aids to buy, it occurred to Frank that he could ask the pharmacist for whatever pet owners gave to their animals when they were taking them on long trips. The pharmacist went directly to the shelf, picked up a package, and said, "This one is the best!"

A few minutes before ten o'clock the Hardy boys were waiting in front of the hotel. Joe was holding the canvas bag containing the fold-up shovel, a flashlight, and a bag of ground pork that had been mixed with some of the sleep aid.

Isabel pulled up in front of the hotel a couple minutes after ten o'clock, but she was driving a dark-colored late-model Ford instead of the Porsche.

Frank and Joe spotted Isabel in the car and quickly climbed in.

"Where's *your* car?" Joe asked.

"I thought it would be too obvious," Isabel explained. "This was the car Father used when we were in the United States. It's in great condition and it doesn't stand out."

"Good thinking," Frank said.

Even though the traffic was heavy, with Isabel's expert driving they made the trip in forty-five minutes. They parked the car two blocks away from Senhora Bragança's house.

"We have about fifteen minutes to prepare," Frank whispered as the three of them climbed out of Isabel's car. "That's plenty of time. Come on."

As they headed toward Senhora Bragança's house Joe explained to Isabel their plan to enter the grounds behind the car that would be carrying the domestic help.

"If everything goes according to schedule, the car will be arriving here just a few minutes before eleven," Frank said. "We'll be hiding behind some shrubs beside the gate and we'll follow the car inside."

Joe told Isabel about the ground pork with the mild sedative. "If this doesn't work on the dogs, then—well, do you think you can scramble back over that fence?"

They were close enough to Senhora Bragança's house for Isabel to judge the high fence. "No problem. I took gymnastics for years," she said. "What about you guys?"

Frank grinned. "We're in track and field back at Bayport High School."

Joe glanced up and down the street. He didn't see anybody. As they were all wearing dark clothing, he doubted that they were visible from Senhora de Feira's house.

Frank looked at his watch. "We need to get behind the shrubs," he whispered. "If it's coming, the car with the domestic help should be here any minute."

They had just hidden themselves when headlights appeared at the far end of the street. Within seconds the gates opened and the big car pulled into the driveway.

"Get ready!" Frank whispered.

When the taillights were even with their hiding place, the three teens crouched down and began following the car. Once on the grounds they veered to the right toward some bushes, where they could hide until the occupants of the car were inside the house.

As they reached the bushes, they heard the dogs.

"Shoot—this doesn't look good!" Joe said.

Frank was frantically trying to unwrap the ground pork. "Let's hope they're more interested in this meat than in us."

9 Buried Alive?

Frank decided to wait until the dogs were almost at the bushes to toss out the ground pork laced with the sleep aid. He thought that they were far enough from the automobile that the driver and the passengers wouldn't see him throw out the meat.

There were three dogs—some of the biggest mastiffs he had ever seen. It was tempting to toss out the meat sooner, but Frank forced himself to wait. He could feel Isabel's tight grasp on his arm. It was almost cutting off the circulation.

"Now!" Joe whispered.

Frank waited a couple more seconds before tossing the meat into the yard, out of the line of vision of the people getting out of the car.

"Look!" Joe whispered. "The driver's coming to check out what the dogs are barking at."

"Oh, great," Frank said. "Now we're in trouble."

"What are we going to do?" Isabel whispered.

"We'll just play it by ear," Frank said. "If he finds us, we'll tell him it's a prank—our climbing over the fence—and that we're sorry. Joe and I can act like crazy teenagers. If he ever watches any of those American television sitcoms, then maybe he'll believe our act!"

"That might work," Isabel said. "I'll use my American accent."

"Rodrigo, come back here now and help us!" a voice called from the vicinity of the car. "You're not going to get out of carrying these bags inside."

The driver muttered several sentences in Portuguese, stopped, scanned the area where the Hardy boys and Isabel were hiding, and then turned and started back to the car.

"What'd he say?" Joe asked Isabel.

"He thinks the dogs must have cornered some kind of animal," Isabel replied. "He also doesn't like these two women. He wishes Senhora Bragança would fire them." She smirked.

When the driver was finally back at the car and listening to the rantings of the two women, Frank exhaled. "Whoa—that was close."

For the next few minutes Frank, Joe, and Isabel

watched as Rodrigo and the two women carried several paper bags into the house. They also kept an eye out for the mastiffs, who had hungrily devoured all of the ground pork.

By the time Rodrigo and the women were finished unloading the car and were finally inside Senhora Bragança's house, the mastiffs were sleeping. They had simply lain down where Frank had tossed the meat and gone to sleep.

"It worked!" Isabel said.

"Yeah, Frank, good plan," Joe said, "but we need to get away from the driveway before the other shift leaves for the night."

"You're right," Frank said. He shone the flashlight on the map that Frau Rilke had drawn. "Let's orient ourselves." On the map he found the location of the driveway, which was nearby. "Frau Rilke even drew in the bushes around us," he said. "Maybe the backyard hasn't changed all that much."

"It's been almost sixty years," Joe said. "Do you think that's possible?"

"Yes, it's possible because Europeans don't change things as much as Americans do," Isabel said. "We have buildings here in Lisbon that are several hundred years old. We'd never think of tearing them down to build new ones, like you sometimes do in the United States."

"That's good for us," Frank said. He turned off the flashlight. "Let's take a look around and see if the rest of the backyard is the same as it was during World War II."

The three of them slowly moved away from the bushes and walked deeper into the backyard, but they kept as close to the fence, the trees, and the shrubs as possible just in case they needed to dash for cover.

Frank had memorized the map that Frau Rilke had drawn for them. Both the moonlight and the security lighting helped them to see where they were going.

"If I'm reading the map correctly," Frank said, "the suitcase is buried between two rosebushes toward the far end of the backyard."

"That's the way I read it too," Joe whispered.

Just then Frank thought he heard voices nearby, so the three of them took cover behind the closest bush. But it turned out to be just an elderly couple taking a stroll on the sidewalk that was adjacent to the fence.

Finally the teens made it to the rear of the backyard. Once again Frank turned on the flashlight so he could see the map.

"The rear of the fence is here, these bushes and shrubs are here," Frank said, pointing to the paper, "and right here, between these two rosebushes, is where Herr Fleissner buried the suitcase." He pointed to the X on the map. "I think we're standing on the spot."

Joe set the canvas bag down on the ground. "We need to get started. We don't have any time to waste."

Frank pointed the flashlight at the ground between the two rosebushes. Joe unfolded the shovel and started digging.

"I get a turn too," Isabel said. "I stay in shape, so I can dig."

"Don't worry, Isabel," Frank said with a grin. "We'll give you a turn!"

"This ground is as hard as a rock," Joe said after he had been digging for about fifteen minutes. "I should have brought some gloves. I don't know why I didn't think about that. I've already got a blister on one of my hands."

"Let me dig for a while," Isabel said.

Joe handed her the shovel. "Be my guest," he said.

Isabel dug for another fifteen minutes, but they had moved only a few inches of soil.

"If I didn't know better," Isabel said, "I'd think we were trying to dig through concrete."

"Let me have a turn," Frank said. He handed the flashlight to Joe.

After fifteen more minutes Frank had made a little progress, but they still weren't down far enough to reach a suitcase that had been buried years ago. "I think the ground's getting softer, though," Frank said as he once again handed the shovel to Joe.

"How much time do you think we have before the dogs wake up?" Isabel asked.

"I don't know," Frank said. "I didn't check the directions on the bottle, because I didn't think we'd have to worry about the lasting power of the pills."

"We've been here for over an hour. We're getting close to the limit, I think," Joe said. He put his left foot on the shovel and pushed it into the earth. "You're right, Frank! It's definitely softer now."

Joe felt he was suddenly making progress, so he began shoveling as fast as he could.

After about ten minutes the shovel struck something hard. "I think we've found it!" Joe said. Using his hands, he brushed away some of the dirt. "It looks like the side of a metal suitcase." He stood up and started shoveling the soil away from the edges of the suitcase. "It shouldn't be too much longer," he whispered.

Frank suddenly felt movement behind him. When he shone the flashlight in that direction, it lit up Antonio de Feira's face. Within seconds Paulo and Rafael had joined him.

"Keep digging," Antonio said. He was pointing a gun at them. "The hole needs to be big enough for the bodies of three young people!"

10 Escape!

Now two more flashlights, held by Paulo and Rafael, were aimed at them.

"Shine them closer to the ground!" Antonio hissed. "If you don't, someone from Senhora Bragança's house will notice!"

"So what?" Paulo said. "We'll just tell them that we're checking on the plants."

"That's a dumb excuse," Joe said. "They'll never believe you."

"Why not? It's our job," Rafael said. "We work as Senhora Bragança's gardeners."

"Not for long," Antonio said angrily. "With this gold we'll finance the fascist revolution in Portugal, and people like Senhora Bragança will work for *us*!"

"We knew that something was up when we didn't

see the dogs," Rafael said. "We wondered what had happened, so we looked for them and found them sound asleep." He laughed. "We've used that trick before ourselves."

Joe suddenly felt as if he were in the middle of some old war movie he had seen on television.

"You'll never get away with burying us alive," Frank said. "People will come looking for us."

"Really? Well, this suitcase has been buried for over sixty years!" Antonio said. "I think it might be another sixty years before anyone finds your skeletons."

"My father is Inspector Manuel Oliveira of the Lisbon Police Department," Isabel said. "You'll be in serious trouble if anything happens to us."

Paulo snickered. "We'll be long gone before he finds you," he said.

"Oh, really?" Isabel said. "Well, for your information, he knows where I am at this very minute. I told him at dinner, right before I came over here." She looked at Frank and Joe. "I'm sorry, guys, but I just had to tell him. I could never do something like this without my father's approval."

"I guess you did what you had to do," Joe said.

Frank could see that Isabel's revelation had an effect on the de Feira brothers' plans.

While Antonio kept the gun aimed at the Hardy boys and Isabel, Paulo and Rafael whispered to each other. When they finished Paulo said, "Well, that just may have saved your life—but I'm sure your father won't be coming to check on you for several hours. So I suggest that you keep digging."

"We just have one shovel," Frank said.

"You have hands, don't you?" Antonio said. "Do you think you're too good to dig with them?"

"I guess not," Frank said. He tried to give the shovel to Isabel so he and Joe would dig with their hands, but Isabel ignored him and said, "What are you going to do with us now after we finish digging?"

"Just be quiet and dig," Rafael said angrily. "You'll find out soon enough."

Isabel took the shovel from Frank and started tossing dirt out of the hole. Frank and Joe got down on their knees and used their hands to dig the soil away from the edges of the metal suitcase.

"What if we made a lot of noise?" Joe whispered to Frank, their voices covered by Isabel's digging. "Do you think that anyone in the house would hear us?"

"It doesn't matter, Joe," Frank whispered back. "Antonio would probably shoot us before help could arrive."

"Well, it looks like Isabel's father was wrong about the de Feira brothers' not being violent," Joe said.

"That's for sure," Frank said.

Joe could see that Isabel was getting tired, so he stood up and said, "Let me have the shovel. You dig with your hands."

As Isabel handed the shovel to Joe, he leaned close enough to her to whisper, "Just pretend to dig. We're trying to come up with a plan."

"Okay," Isabel whispered back.

As if on cue, Frank said, "Hey, de Feiras! The dirt down here is like concrete. It'll take *forever* to get this suitcase out of here."

Joe looked up to see the de Feiras' reaction and saw that Antonio was folding up a cell phone. "I just had a conversation with a friend of mine at the Lisbon Police Department," he said. "Inspector Oliveira has been in Porto all day. There is no way you could have had dinner with your father before you came over here, Senorita Oliveira. You weren't telling the truth, were you?"

Isabel gave the de Feiras a hard look, then picked up some dirt and threw it at them. It fell short of reaching the brothers. "I'll not dig anymore!" she said.

"Don't antagonize them, Isabel," Frank whispered. "We'll figure out some way to get out of here."

Isabel knelt back down and started digging. "I'm sorry, I really am," she said. "I thought if I lied to them about telling my father, they might let us go, but it didn't work." She looked at Frank. "Do you think we can get out of here alive?" she whispered.

"We've always been able to find some way out of

every bad situation," Joe said, "and we don't plan to give up now."

Paulo and Rafael kept their flashlights aimed into the hole where the Hardy boys and Isabel were digging.

It took them almost thirty more minutes before Joe whispered, "I think I've reached the bottom of the suitcase on my side."

"Me too. Let's see if we can get our fingers under it and move it," Frank said. He looked up at Paulo and Rafael. "That light is causing my eyes to tear up, making it hard for me to dig. We're almost there, I think—so could you just shine it away for a while?"

Paulo and Rafael grunted but didn't argue. They shone the flashlights on the ground at the edge of the hole, leaving the Hardy boys and Isabel in darkness.

"Isabel, continue digging," Frank whispered. "I want the de Feiras to think we still have a long way to go yet."

While Isabel dug, Frank and Joe were able to get their fingers under the suitcase and move it.

"Okay, it's a little heavier than I thought it would be, but I think we can get it out now," Frank said. "We have to figure out how to make sure this suitcase leaves with *us*, though, and *not* with the de Feira brothers."

"Frank, you pick it up—then I'll jump out of the hole and take the suitcase from you," Joe whispered.

"Once I have it, maybe I can say something like, 'Tell me where you want me to take it.' Knowing how the de Feiras feel about being other people's servants, maybe they'll like it if somebody is doing the hard work for them."

"Good thinking, Joe—but where is all of this going to end up?" Frank said. "You don't want to take the suitcase where they tell you to take it."

"No, you're right. That's where Isabel's acting comes in," Joe whispered. He leaned closer to Isabel. "Somewhere closer to the house, where we can be heard, I want you to fake some kind of an attack— like a stomachache or something. Roll around on the ground if you have to."

"That'll be easy," Isabel said. "I did that in a commercial once."

At that moment Paulo and Rafael turned the flashlights back on them.

"We heard you whispering," Paulo said. "What's going on?"

Joe stood up. "I'll tell you what's going on," he said. "We're ready to move the suitcase."

That caused excitement among the de Feira brothers. Joe was able to climb out of the hole and say, "Hand it to me, Frank. I'll carry it wherever the de Feiras want me to."

Frank struggled to lift the suitcase out of the hole, but he finally managed it. Joe grabbed the handle, but it immediately pulled away. The leather had rotted. The suitcase tumbled over on its side.

"Open it!" Antonio said. "I want to see that gold for myself."

Joe reached down and tried to unfasten the catches on the suitcase, but they were rusted shut. "I'm going to need some tools," he said.

"We don't have time for this," Rafael said. "We'll open it after we get it back to headquarters."

"Pick it up," Paulo said to Joe.

Frank came to the rescue with, "Let me help you, Joe. It looks as though you'll need another hand. I'll grab one end and you grab the other."

Almost before the de Feiras realized what was happening, Frank and Joe had started to carry the heavy metal suitcase in the direction of Senhora Bragança's house. Isabel was right behind them.

Suddenly Paulo grabbed Frank around the throat. "Where do you think you're going?" he hissed.

"We're carrying the suitcase out for you," Joe said. "Isn't that what you wanted?"

"We're not going that way. We've got our truck parked behind the rear gate," Antonio said. "The servants' entrance," he added with a snarl. "That's where we want you to carry it."

Oh, no! Joe thought. *We'll be getting farther and farther away from people who might be able to help us.*

Initially Frank thought that he and Joe might be able to make a run for it, even with the heavy suitcase. When Antonio brandished his gun, though, Frank knew that he and Joe would have to follow the men's orders.

Joe suddenly reminded himself of the de Feira brothers' original plan: to bury the three of them in the pit where the suitcase had been. He realized that they might still have that plan in mind.

With Paulo and Rafael leading the way with their flashlights, Frank and Joe carried the metal suitcase farther and farther toward the rear of Senhora Bragança's backyard.

Antonio had the gate open and was standing beside an old truck. "Put it in the back," he commanded.

Frank and Joe heaved the suitcase onto the bed of the old truck.

"I hope you're happy now," Isabel said. She started to walk away, heading back toward Senhora Bragança's house as if that was the most normal thing in the world to do. Paulo grabbed her by the arm, though. "Nice try," he said, "but we have other plans for the three of you."

"What?" Frank demanded.

"Weren't you listening earlier?" Rafael said.

"Yeah!" Antonio said. "If that suitcase can stay buried for over sixty years, there's no reason why the three of you can't stay buried just as long."

"I don't care what that person told you," Isabel protested. "I had dinner with my father and told him where I was going."

"Start walking back to the pit," Antonio said.

It was useless to try anything in the alley, Frank decided, because they were too far away from the house. The area where the suitcase had been buried still wasn't very close, but at least it was on the grounds. They had to hope for a miracle.

For almost the first time in his life Joe could think of no way out of their current predicament. He couldn't imagine what lay ahead of them. He would have to submit to either being buried alive or, if he cried out, being shot by one of the de Feira brothers. These seemed to be his only alternatives.

But just as they reached the rosebushes Isabel fell down and started screaming, "My stomach! My stomach! Oh, please help me. It hurts so much!"

Frank and Joe took up the cry. "You've got to do something. This has happened to her before. It's her appendix!"

It was obvious that the de Feira brothers were totally unprepared for something like this.

At that moment Isabel let out a blood-curdling scream so loud that it caused both Frank and Joe to wince.

Suddenly lights flicked on at the back of Senhora

Bragança's house and voices cried out in Portuguese.

Isabel screamed again, this time even louder—and Frank thought that would have been impossible.

"Let's get out of here!" Antonio said.

He started running back toward the rear of the yard. Paulo and Rafael were right behind him.

Isabel jumped up. "How was that?" she said.

Frank looked at her. "Very convincing," he managed to say. "Are you sure you're okay?"

"Perfectly," Isabel said. "But I don't want to be caught trespassing. Come on!"

Voices from Senhora Bragança's house were getting closer.

"They've called the police," Isabel translated. "They're also trying to find the dogs." She was leading them along the far side of the fence—not away from Senhora Bragança's house but toward it.

"Are you sure we're going in the right direction?" Frank asked.

"Trust me," Isabel said. "This is just like a movie I was in once."

After a few minutes Joe relaxed because, as Isabel had predicted, the voices were getting less and less distinct.

"Now, *this* is the hard part," Isabel said. "We're going to have to escape through the house."

Frank stopped. "Are you nuts? They'll catch us for sure."

"I think Frank's right," Joe said. "We need to get out another way."

"Look, guys, think about it," Isabel said. "Where are all the people looking for us?"

Frank and Joe looked at each other.

"Outside," Frank said.

"Exactly," Isabel said. "So doesn't it stand to reason that we should be *inside*?"

Joe shrugged. "Well, it's hard to argue with that, I guess."

Isabel smiled. "We'll go out the front door like any other guest," she said.

With that she led the Hardy boys up the rear steps of the house and through the back door.

No one was around, although they could hear voices somewhere in the house.

"From here on it's just guesswork," Isabel said. "If anyone stops us, we'll just act as if we know what we're doing."

Slowly and stealthily they made their way, from room to room, through Senhora Bragança's house. They ducked in and out of rooms all the way to the front of the house, and only once they narrowly missed being seen by a member of the household staff.

Finally they reached the front door. Just as they exited the house, though, they heard a car squealing out of the de Feiras' driveway across the street—and they ducked behind some shrubs so that the de Feiras wouldn't see them.

When the taillights had disappeared, Isabel said, "Now then, we need to get out of here and start making plans to get that gold back!"

11 Danger on the River

Joe looked over at the de Feira house. "There are no lights," he said. "I guess everyone was in the car."

"They may have abandoned the house and gone into hiding," Frank suggested, "now that they have all that gold."

"Why would they abandon their house?" Isabel said.

"It's falling apart," Joe told her. "They probably haven't done anything to it in years."

"It's kind of sad, really," Isabel said. "Getting all that gold is probably the only thing Senhora de Feira has had on her mind for over sixty years."

"It probably started right after Frau Rilke told her about it," Frank said.

"You know," Joe said, "that's going to make it even harder for us to find the gold."

"Right," Frank said. "There's no telling where the de Feiras were headed."

Just as they reached Isabel's car several police cars passed them on the street and converged in Senhora Bragança's driveway.

"They probably just discovered the hole," Frank said. "If Senhora Bragança puts two and two together, she'll know it has something to do with the story we told her about Frau Rilke."

"And she'll probably tell the police that two American teenagers came by the other day, asking her suspicious questions," Joe added.

"That means the police may be waiting for us when we get back to the hotel," Frank said.

"Maybe not," Isabel said as she started the car and made a u-turn to head back toward central Lisbon. "For all we know, someone at Senhora Bragança's house might have spotted the de Feiras leaving the grounds, then saw their car speeding away. They may think they're the ones responsible for the hole in the backyard."

"That would be too good to be true," Joe said. "To have the Lisbon police do all of our work for us!"

"Yeah, but if the Lisbon police find the de Feira brothers," Frank reminded him, "they'll also find the suitcase with the gold bars, and that won't help Frau Rilke at all."

"You're right," Joe said. "I doubt if we could just walk into the police station and say, 'Excuse me, but that suitcase belongs to a friend of ours in the United States. We're here to claim it for her.'"

"I see what you mean," Isabel said. "That wouldn't work."

"We just have to hope that the police aren't looking for us," Frank said, "and that if they *are* looking for the de Feiras, they don't find them."

"I wouldn't worry. This is probably at the bottom of the department's list of things to investigate," Isabel said. "Unfortunately the Lisbon Police Department is like police departments all over the world: overworked!"

Isabel dropped the Hardy boys off in front of the hotel and told them she'd call the next day after her audition for a Portuguese soap opera. "I'm very excited about it," she said. "I'm trying out for the role of a *really* bad person." She laughed. "Of course, it'll call for a lot of acting, as it's totally out of character for me!"

Frank and Joe grinned.

"Thanks for all you did for us tonight, Isabel," Frank said.

"Yeah—we appreciate the help," Joe added.

"Well, it's not over yet, guys," Isabel said. "I'll start thinking about where the de Feiras might have taken the gold." She raised an eyebrow. "Being the daughter of a high-ranking police officer has its perks," she added. "I *do* have my own contacts within the police department!"

"We need all the help you can give us, Isabel," Joe said. "We just don't want to return to Bayport empty-handed. Frau Rilke and her family are really counting on us to return the family fortune to them."

As the Hardy boys headed into the hotel they saw their parents and Aunt Gertrude coming out of the hotel newsstand.

"Postcard time," Joe whispered to Frank. "I'm sure of it."

"Hello, boys! I was wondering if you were back yet," Mrs. Hardy called out. When she reached her sons, she added, "After the movie we went to a wonderful little restaurant for a late supper. We weren't tired yet. I guess we're *still* on Bayport time."

"Actually, we just got here," Frank said. "Isabel brought us back."

"What a nice young lady she is," Aunt Gertrude said, winking at the boys.

Frank and Joe smirked in return.

"What did you just buy, Mom?" Joe asked.

"Postcards," Mrs. Hardy replied. "Your aunt and I promised a lot of people we'd send them a card from Lisbon, and if we don't get them mailed tomorrow, we'll beat them back to Bayport."

Joe winked at Frank.

"Did everything go all right?" Mr. Hardy asked, giving his sons a knowing look.

With their eyes Frank and Joe told him that it didn't, but so as not to worry his mother, Frank said, "As well as could be expected. We need to talk to you about it later."

"Okay," Fenton Hardy said. "Let me take a shower and then I'll come over to your room while your mother and aunt write their postcards."

While they were waiting for their father, Frank and Joe got ready for bed.

By the time Mr. Hardy finally arrived, Joe had already dozed off and Frank was yawning—so Frank gave his father an abbreviated account of what had happened at Senhora Bragança's house.

"I don't really like this, Frank," Mr. Hardy said. "Those people are dangerous."

"We know that now, Dad," Frank said. "We made the same mistake a lot of people in Europe made when Hitler's thugs first started causing trouble." He shook his head. "We thought they weren't serious."

Mr. Hardy nodded. "We can't allow that to happen again." He stood up. "Before you guys do anything else, let me do a little checking around," he said. "I guess I should have done this in the first place, but I honestly thought it would be better to locate the gold first, *then* talk to the authorities about how to get it out of the country."

Joe turned over. Mr. Hardy grinned at Frank. "You'd better get some sleep," he said.

"Okay, Dad," Frank said. "See you in the morning."

When the telephone rang the next morning, Frank answered it still half-asleep. So Mr. Hardy said, "Well, I guess that means you guys won't be joining us for breakfast."

"I'm more tired than I thought I would be," Frank said, "and Joe's still conked out. I guess the answer is no."

"Well, just remember what I said about the gold," Mr. Hardy reminded him. "Don't do anything else about it until I've done some work. Okay?"

"No problem, Dad," Frank said. "In fact, I had a dream about renting a motorboat and taking it out on the Tagus River today—just like we've done in Barmet Bay back home."

"That's a great idea," Mr. Hardy said. "I noticed several different boats on the river the other day. I imagine it would be a nice way to see the city."

"Great," Frank told him. "Enjoy breakfast!"

After Frank hung up he called the concierge and asked him about renting a motorboat for a cruise on the Tagus River later in the day. It turned out that the travel bureau in the hotel could take care of all the arrangements for them.

"All you'll need to do is stop by on your way out and sign an agreement," the concierge said. "It's simple—people do it all the time."

By the time Frank and Joe were ready, so was the motorboat.

The woman in the travel bureau told them that it would be easiest to take a taxi to the docks where they'd be getting the boat.

"You could take the bus, but why would you want to? A taxi is so much faster," she said.

"I guess she assumes that if we have enough money to rent a motorboat, then we must have enough money to pay for a taxi," Joe said as they left the hotel and indicated to the doorman that they needed a taxi.

"She's right, though, because we're on a definite schedule," Frank said. "The first time we went to Belém, I didn't want to call attention to our arrival—and we had all the time we wanted."

It only took the doorman a minute to get a taxi for the teens. As Joe handed a tip to the doorman, he noticed two men push a couple of women out of the way and jump into one of the taxis behind them. "Frank, don't look now, but I think we have company," he whispered as the taxi pulled out into traffic.

"What do you mean?" Frank asked.

Joe told his brother what he had seen. "I don't think they were just being rude, either," he said, "because they had on the same kind of clothes as what the de Feira brothers wear—different colors but same style."

"Why would anybody be following us *now*?" Frank said. "We don't have the gold anymore."

"That's what I'm wondering," Joe said.

"Well, they can follow us for all I care. They're not going to get anything," Frank said. "All I'm interested in now is taking a motorboat out on the Tagus and seeing the sights."

Joe positioned himself in the back of the taxi so that he could look in the driver's rearview mirror. After they had driven several blocks and made a few sharp turns, the taxi with the two men was still behind them.

"They're not giving up easily, Frank," Joe said.

"Too bad," Frank said. Inwardly, though, he was a little worried. *What if they follow us onto the river?* he wondered. *What then?* "I'm not going to be intimidated," he said, "but we should both be alert just in case."

Finally the taxi pulled up in front of the Cais do Sodré tram station, which also served as a port for ferries heading to Cacilhas. "You get the motorboats just to the left," the driver said. "You'll see the signs inside."

"Thanks," Frank said, handing over the amount of money on the meter plus a tip—even though he had been told that taxi drivers in Portugal didn't expect tips.

As Frank and Joe exited their taxi, the taxi that had been following them drove past. Frank and Joe watched it disappear down the street.

"I guess they're not going to hassle us after all," Joe said. "They probably just wanted to know where we were going."

"I still don't understand this," Frank said. "We don't have the gold. Why are they following us?"

As they started into the station Joe said, "Maybe they don't know that the de Feiras stole the gold from us, Frank."

"Well, if they know about us, wouldn't they also know what the de Feira brothers did?" Frank said. "Information like this seems to have a way of getting broadcast to all of the criminal elements in a country. They have quite a network."

Joe shrugged. "It looks like we're not going to have to worry about them now, anyway," he said.

Once inside the station, they saw a sign that pointed to the motorboat rental office. The man behind the counter was quite friendly, spoke English, and had the boat keys waiting for the teens.

"Your American marine operator's licenses and your insurance coverage are also good in Portugal," he said, "and since this is an American motorboat, I'm sure you're quite familiar with how to operate it. It's company policy, however, that I explain everything about the boat to you—and also give you information about the other boat traffic and the currents on the Tagus."

"We have a boat just like this back in Bayport," Joe told him, "but we certainly understand your company's policy."

The motorboat was berthed at the end of the pier and looked as though it had been well cared for.

"I'm glad we decided to do this, Frank," Joe said. "We need to take some mental space from that case."

The man kept the instructions at a professional level, given what Joe had told him about their motorboat back in Bayport. After Frank and Joe both took a look at the navigation map of the Tagus and asked several questions about the river, Frank saw the man relax noticeably. He was clearly convinced that he didn't need to worry about the two teenagers bringing the boat back safely.

The man headed back up the dock, saluted to the Hardy boys, and turned back to the rental office.

Joe started the engine, backed the motorboat out of its berth, and headed out onto the Tagus.

Their plan was to go upriver as far as the new Ponte Vasco da Gama, then back down the Tagus under the Ponte 25 de Abril, and as far as Belém.

"This is easy," Joe said. "These different-colored buoys will keep us from getting into trouble with the rest of the boat traffic."

"Ah, this is the life, isn't it?" Frank said. He had sat down in the seat next to Joe, laced his fingers together behind his head, and leaned back.

"You're telling . . . ," Joe started to say, when they heard a cracking sound. Suddenly the boat's windshield shattered. "What the . . ."

Frank turned around. Behind them they saw another motorboat with two men in it—and it was gaining speed. One man was driving the boat and the other was aiming a rifle in their direction.

"Somebody's shooting at us, Joe!" Frank said.

12 Where Is Frau Rilke's Gold?

"Quick, Frank—look at that navigation map!" Joe shouted. "I think there's another dock up the river. We need to head for it ASAP!"

Frank leaned down to pick up the navigation map just as a bullet whizzed over his head. He dropped to the floor. "Joe, you need to start moving the boat in a zigzag," he said. "If you don't, one of those bullets is going to hit its mark."

Right away Joe began to weave the motorboat through the water, regardless of the buoys. This was no time to worry about anything except escaping. "See anything on the map?" he shouted.

Frank glanced down at the map, then scanned the shore of the Tagus. "Yes! I think that's the Doca do Terreiro do Trigo," he said, pointing ahead. "You need to go that way."

Joe, still zigzagging, headed the motorboat roughly toward the dock.

"You're doing a great job dodging bullets," Frank shouted. "Nothing has . . ." Just then a bullet hit the gas tank, and fuel began leaking onto the floor of the boat. "Joe—I think I spoke too soon!"

"If a bullet hits the gasoline, it could cause the boat to explode," Joe shouted. "And we're too far from the dock to take a chance on trying to make it to shore!"

"I guess that means only one thing," Frank said. "We'll have to swim the rest of the way. Are you up to it?"

"The same thing happened to us once in Barmet Bay—remember? We made it to shore then, as rough as that water was. So this should be no problem," Joe said. "I'll cut the engine so that we don't go much farther and destroy something in our path."

Frank looked at the approaching motorboat. It was still several yards away. "Joe, if there were some way we could slip over the side, unnoticed, and swim underwater before they get here, then I think we might have a chance," he said.

Joe looked at the other motorboat. "Hey—looks like they're slowing down," he said. "Maybe they think we're going to spring some kind of trap on them."

"Let them think what they want to," Joe said. "This pause should give us enough time to be far away from this boat before they decide to get closer."

Joe turned the motorboat around so that the windshield, though shattered in several places, would hide them as they slipped into the river. "I hadn't thought about it, Frank, but probably *this* even looks a little threatening," he said. "They may think we're going to take a run at them."

"We may just survive this after all," Frank said.

The teens quickly took off their shoes, secured their wallets in their clothes as well as they could, and slipped over the side of the motorboat into the murky water.

"I think the river is just muddy, not polluted," Frank said, "so we should be able to swim underwater until we're far enough from the boat to escape detection."

Frank and Joe each took several deep breaths before heading underwater toward the dock.

Frank was sure they hadn't swum more than fifty yards when he felt a shockwave. It forced him to the surface. He couldn't believe what he saw— their motorboat had exploded. Pieces of it were starting to fall into the water around them.

Joe surfaced and took a gulp of air.

"Dive! Dive!" Frank screamed at him.

Several large chunks of what used to be the boat were headed right for Joe's head.

Joe glanced up, saw what was happening, and dove underwater just in time to save himself.

Frank dove right after his brother and forced himself to keep his eyes open. It caused a momentary stinging sensation, but Frank could at least see far enough to know that Joe was okay.

Joe swam as fast as he could, checking his direction each time he came up for air. He wanted to make sure he was headed directly for the docks and *not* back out into the middle of the Tagus. Frank was right behind him.

When Frank surfaced again, he heard sirens from what he was sure were police boats converging on the scene of the accident. Frank stopped swimming and started treading water. He looked back in the direction of the enemy boat and saw nothing. *Of course,* he thought, *they're not about to stay around and explain why they were shooting at the Hardys' boat.*

Joe had now surfaced and was also treading water. He waved to Frank and Frank waved back. Then Joe pointed to the police boat that was headed toward them. "Let's keep our story simple," he shouted to Frank. "There's no need to complicate matters."

"Good idea," Frank shouted back.

The police boat first reached Joe, took him aboard, and then picked up Frank. A police officer handed each of them a blanket and then gave them each a small cup of very strong coffee.

"I told them I didn't speak Portuguese," Joe whispered. "I don't think any of them speak much English."

Within minutes they had reached the building that housed the river police. Frank and Joe were taken to a room, given dry blankets, and told in Portuguese and some English to wait until an English-speaking police officer could be located.

Finally a man named Captain Matos arrived. He greeted the teens pleasantly in English and then apologized profusely for the accident, telling them that he was just glad that two American citizens weren't killed while on a pleasure cruise down the Tagus River.

"So are we," Frank said.

"Sometimes these rental motorboats aren't maintained properly," Captain Matos said. "Of course, this could have just been an unfortunate accident."

"You just never know what to expect," Joe said lamely. He had to admit that he wasn't prepared for such a simple solution to what had happened. "What do we do now?"

"There's not much we can do," Captain Matos

said. "I'll have one of our officers drop you off at your hotel and you can get cleaned up. We'll take care of all of the paperwork here." He gave them a big smile. "Again, I'm just glad that you're okay."

Still wrapped in blankets, the Hardy boys were taken to a car that was parked just outside the front entrance to the police station. Captain Matos opened the door for them, and Frank and Joe climbed into the backseat.

"Take these young men to the Hotel Lisboa Plaza," Captain Matos said to the driver.

"Thanks, Captain Matos," Joe said.

"My pleasure," Captain Matos said. He closed the door and nodded at the driver.

As the driver pulled out into traffic Frank leaned over as if he were trying to adjust the blanket around his shoulders. He managed to get close enough to Joe's ear to whisper, "Don't say anything at all."

Frank nodded, then leaned forward. "How far are we from our hotel?" he asked the driver.

"We're in the Alfama. Your hotel is in the Baixa, not far from the Bairro Alto," the driver said. "Maybe five kilometers?"

"Thanks," Frank said. "I wasn't sure."

He looked out the window to see if he could read the street signs. He saw that they were on the Avenida Infante Dom Henrique. He knew that this street was a major thoroughfare. *Well,* he thought, *as long as we don't turn off onto some deserted road, we'll be fine.*

When the driver turned right onto the Rua Aurea, Frank felt they were probably going to be all right. He knew that this street led directly to the Avenida da Liberdade.

Finally the driver pulled up in front of their hotel.

"We'll just leave the blankets in the car," Frank said. "We're still a little wet, but we'll look less obvious without them."

"Okay," the driver said.

"Thanks for the ride," Frank said.

"Yeah, thanks," Joe said.

Once the boys were out of the car, the driver pulled back into traffic, and Frank and Joe headed for the front door of the hotel.

"Okay, I want to know a couple of things," Joe said. "First of all, why didn't you want me to say anything? And second of all, why were you so nervous on the trip back? Are you worried that we'll have to pay for the boat?"

"Did you tell Captain Matos where we were staying?" Frank said.

Joe stopped. "No, I didn't, but . . . he knew, didn't he? He told the driver where to take us."

"Exactly," Frank said. He pushed the button for

the elevator. "I thought that whole interview was a bit too simple. So I'm thinking he's connected in some way to what happened."

"Are you telling me that you think he's one of the fascists too?" Joe said.

When the elevator car arrived, the teens stepped back to let the passengers off.

On the way up to their floor, Frank said, "I'm just saying that I don't know whom to trust anymore. He knew more than we told him and he clearly didn't want a big investigation."

"Well, what I want to do first is get out of these wet clothes and have something to eat," Joe said, inserting the key into the door of their room. The telephone rang just as they entered. "Hurry! It might be Mom or Dad, wondering where we are. If they know we had a second close call, we'll probably be on the next plane to Bayport."

Joe quickly grabbed the receiver. "Hello?"

"We want that gold and we want it now," the voice said. "We're tired of playing games with you."

"Well, I've got news for you," Joe managed to say calmly. He motioned for Frank to move near the receiver. "The de Feira brothers have the gold."

"We're sure that's what you wanted everybody to think," the voice said. "But the de Feira brothers have a suitcase full of bricks."

13 The German Soldier

Joe hung up the receiver. "That guy has to be telling the truth, Frank," he said. "Why would he call us and tell us something like that?"

Frank nodded. "I think you're right, Joe. It also makes sense. Isabel's source—who said the information about the suitcase with the gold bars had made its way through the underworld network—was probably right on the mark."

"Maybe those people who were shooting at us on the river just meant to scare us," Joe offered. "Maybe they didn't mean to hit the gas tank."

"That fits too," Frank said. "We both agree that they're dangerous, but that doesn't stop them from making mistakes."

"That's the truth," Joe said. He let out a big sigh.

"What now?"

"We call Isabel and let her know what's going on," Frank said.

"Good idea," Joe said. He picked up the receiver again and dialed Isabel's number.

When Isabel answered, Joe told her about what had happened on the Tagus and then about the telephone call they had just received. "What do you make of it?" he asked.

"I agree with your assessment," Isabel said. "There really must have been bricks in the suitcase, or they wouldn't have called you."

"How did the bricks get there?" Joe said.

"I have a feeling that Senhora Bragança knows more about the gold than we thought," Isabel said, "but I also have a feeling she'd never tell."

"You may be right," Joe said.

"So you must be very careful now. I don't think you should leave the hotel—there are probably a lot of people out there who think you still have the gold," Isabel continued. "They could try to kidnap you and coerce the information out of you somehow."

"That doesn't sound pretty," Joe said.

"Let me talk to some of my father's undercover police officers," Isabel said. "They should know what's going on."

"Okay," Joe said. "We'll just stay here until we hear from you."

Joe hung up the phone and relayed the entire conversation to Frank.

"While you were talking to Isabel, I was thinking about Senhora Bragança," Frank said. "I agree with Isabel. I think she knows something about that suitcase. You saw the way she looked when we mentioned the person who had previously lived in that house."

Joe nodded. "Do you think she found the gold and then put the bricks in the suitcase, so that it would look like she hadn't stolen the treasure?" he asked.

"Well, at first, I'd actually thought that might be what had happened," Frank said, "but then I thought it had to be somebody else—somebody Senhora Bragança allowed to dig up the suitcase."

"She wouldn't let just anybody do that, Frank," Joe said. "It would have to be somebody . . ." He stopped. "Hey—are you thinking what I'm thinking?"

"If you're thinking that maybe the German soldier didn't die after all," Frank said, "then I sure am."

"But how could that be, Frank?" Joe said. "Frau Rilke said that her father saw the Gestapo officer kidnap the soldier in downtown Lisbon."

"That's right," Frank agreed. "But what she *didn't* say is that they received confirmation of his death."

"Exactly! And how could they?" Joe said. "They left for the United States almost immediately because they feared the soldier would break under questioning, reveal the hiding place of the gold, and lead the Gestapo to the Fleissner's home."

"A lot of strange things happened during World War II," Frank said. "People survived things that nobody would have thought possible."

"The German soldier could have survived too," Joe said. "If we had his whole name, we might be able to find out exactly what *did* happen to him."

"Frau Rilke gave it to us—but I can't recall the whole name," Frank said. He looked at his watch. "It's still early in Bayport. Let's call her and tell her what we suspect."

It took only fifteen minutes for the hotel operator to get Frau Rilke on the telephone. Frank told her that they still hadn't recovered the gold bars, that they were close—but that some information had come to light that made them believe that perhaps the German soldier hadn't died after all.

"His name is Heinz-Erich Lüdemann," Frau Rilke said. "If he's still alive, it's a miracle—and, of course, if he is, half of the gold bars belong to him. Oh, it would be so wonderful to see Heinz-Erich after all these years!"

"Well, we don't know for sure that he's alive—we're just speculating," Frank reminded her. "But now that we have his full name, we *are* going to do our best to find out what happened to him."

Frank promised Frau Rilke that he would telephone her as soon as they found out something more definite. After he hung up the phone, he turned to his brother. "In the morning we need to let Dad know about this too."

When Mr. Hardy called Frank and Joe the next morning to ask them if they wanted to have breakfast, he was surprised to learn that they were already dressed and waiting for his call.

As everyone headed down to the restaurant Frank and Joe filled Mr. Hardy in on everything that had happened the day before. Since Mrs. Hardy and Aunt Gertrude were several paces behind them, engaged in a discussion about what to do first that morning, Frank and Joe decided to include the part about the exploding boat.

"Now we're thinking that the German soldier didn't die after all, Dad," Joe said. "We called Frau Rilke last night and got his name."

"I think your theory has some merit," Fenton Hardy said. "I have a meeting at the Central Police Station later this morning. I can ask about how to start looking for this Heinz-Erich Lüdemann."

After breakfast Frank and Joe returned to their room, as they had told Isabel they would, while Mr. Hardy went to his meeting and Mrs. Hardy and Aunt Gertrude left to go shopping. After finding nothing on television they were interested in—or could understand—they both decided that they hadn't had enough sleep the night before and that now would be a good time to catch up on it.

Three hours later the telephone awakened them both. Joe picked it up. It was Mr. Hardy.

"Well, right away I was able to find an official who could help me try to locate this Heinz-Erich Lüdemann," he said, "but unfortunately he didn't come up with anything."

"Nothing?" Joe said, crestfallen.

"Nothing," Mr. Hardy repeated. "We even tried a database that contains names in all of the countries in the European Union. There was no Heinz-Erich Lüdemann who would have been a soldier in World War II. Sorry."

"Okay, Dad. Thanks for trying," Joe said. "Talk to you later."

Frank shook his head. "I was certain that would solve the problem for us, Joe," he said. "Now I don't know which way to turn."

Joe slammed his fist into his pillow. "We can't go home empty-handed, Frank. Frau Rilke is counting on us."

"Okay, let's take stock of what we *do* know. And let's forget everything that's happened and put ourselves in Heinz-Erich Lüdemann's shoes for a moment," Frank said. "Maybe that'll help us come up with a new game plan."

"Good idea! You've just been captured by the

Gestapo. You're taken to a really horrible place where people do really horrible things to you," Joe said. "But you will yourself to stay alive. You're not going to let these monsters end your life."

"Right. Now let's say you *do* manage to stay alive until the end of the war, and when the Nazis surrender, you're released," Frank continued. "You have nothing, you're weak from hunger, and your family is all gone."

"What sort of life do you go back to?" Joe said.

Frank jumped up from the bed. "Hang on! I just remembered something I saw in an old black-and-white movie," he said. "This woman was in a concentration camp and she took care of another sick woman. When the sick woman died, the protagonist assumed the other woman's identity because the dead woman had relatives in San Francisco. She'd never seen the relatives, but they'd invited her to come to their home and live with them after the war."

"Heinz-Erich Lüdemann might *not* have returned to life as Heinz-Erich Lüdemann! He might have come back with another name," Joe said.

"Right. The most important things you could have back then were papers that would allow you to cross borders," Frank said. "Let's suppose that somehow he made it back to Portugal because he would want to find out if the Fleissners were still here—and when he found that they weren't, maybe he somehow convinced Senhora Bragança that the suitcase buried in her backyard belonged to him and the people who used to live there. He dug it up and replaced the gold bars with bricks."

"That's what I don't understand," Joe said. "Why would he rebury the suitcase with bricks?"

"To throw the Nazis off track," Frank said.

"What Nazis?" Joe said.

"Joe, after the war there were a lot of Nazis who escaped from Germany and went into hiding all over the world," Frank said. "Let's say that one way or another some of the Nazis who captured Heinz-Erich Lüdemann had a pretty good idea of where the gold might be buried. Maybe they got the information out of him. Maybe Heinz-Erich told somebody he trusted and then that person betrayed him. I don't know. He probably thought that if he reburied the suitcase with bricks, then whoever dug it up might think that it had never contained gold bars in the first place—and that the gold that Heinz-Erich Lüdemann said he had buried there could be almost anywhere. They wouldn't even know where to begin."

"Well, Frank, at least we have a possible solution to what happened to the gold," Joe said, "but how do we find Heinz-Erich Lüdemann without a name?"

Frank picked up the Lisbon telephone directory

and started thumbing through the yellow pages until he found *"Journais."* "Newspapers," he said. "Now, I think there's probably . . . Yes! Here it is. *Die Zeit!*"

"That's German, Frank," Joe said.

"I know, Joe. I got an A in Mrs. Rolf's class last year, remember?" Frank said. "We're going to put a personal ad in Lisbon's German newspaper: *Die Familie Fleissner sucht Heinz-Erich Lüdemann.* The Fleissner family is looking for Heinz-Erich Lüdemann."

"Well, it might work," Joe said. "I bet the concierge could help us do it. He's been able to do everything else for us."

Thirty minutes later Frank and Joe were back in their room with assurances from the concierge that the personal ad would appear in the next morning's edition of Lisbon's German-language newspaper, *Die Zeit,* along with Frank and Joe's hotel telephone number.

"I don't think I can stand just sitting around anymore," Joe said. "I'm feeling restless. I've got to get out of this room."

"You know what Isabel said, Joe," Frank reminded him. "We need to lie low for another day or so. How about working out in the gym? Judging from the picture in the hotel's guest services magazine, it's top-notch."

"That might help," Joe said. "Let's go."

Just then the telephone rang.

"Maybe it's Isabel," Frank said, picking it up. "Hello?"

The voice immediately started speaking in German.

"Wait, wait. Slow down! I don't really *speak* German that well," Frank said frantically. He couldn't believe that someone had already found out about the newspaper ad, but in English he added, "Are you calling about the ad I just placed in *Die Zeit*?"

For just a moment there was silence. Then a woman's voice quietly said, "Perhaps."

"I don't understand. The newspaper hasn't even printed the ad yet," Frank said. "How do you know about it?"

"Lisbon's German community is very close-knit," the woman said. "Someone at the newspaper office called me."

"Okay, then. Please listen carefully. Don't hang up," Frank said. He tried to tell Frau Rilke's story as quickly and as concisely as possible. When he finished, he said, "Do you know Heinz-Erich Lüdemann?"

"I think we should talk," the woman said. "I will meet you but only in public."

"Name the place," Frank said.

"Sua Excêlencia. It's a popular restaurant," the

woman said. She gave Frank the address. "Tonight at eight o'clock. I'll have a table reserved under the name 'Santana.'"

"We'll be there," Frank said.

14 Car Underwater

When Frank got off the telephone with the woman, immediately he called Isabel.

"She wants to meet us at Sua Excêlencia at eight o'clock tonight," he said. "The address is . . ."

"Oh, I know where it is. It's one of Lisbon's nicest restaurants," Isabel said. "I go there a lot. It's not close to your hotel, so I'll drive you."

"Great! Thanks for offering," Frank said. "What time will you pick us up?"

"Half past seven," Isabel said. "That'll give us time to get there, park, and then find this woman."

"See you then," Frank said. He hung up the phone and turned to Joe. "Now if we can just find something to keep us occupied for the rest of the day, we'll be okay."

"The gym!" Joe said. "That'll get rid of some of this excess energy."

"Right," Frank said. "Let's change and head on up there."

For the next couple of hours the Hardy boys worked their way through every piece of equipment in the state-of-the-art gym. By the time they were through, they were exhausted.

"We might have overdone it," Joe said. He looked around the gym. "I wish we had some of this equipment back in Bayport."

"Me too," Frank agreed.

When they got back to their room, they took turns with the shower. Then Frank called guest services and asked for a wake-up call at six o'clock.

"That should give us plenty of time to nap and get ready," he said to Joe.

"I don't know, Frank," Joe said with a yawn. "It may take me that long just to wake up."

But when the wake-up call came, both Frank and Joe bounded out of bed with no trouble and got dressed.

"We'd better call Dad, just to keep him informed," Joe said. "I think he was a little anxious about what happened on the river."

Frank picked up the phone and called their

parents' room. When his father answered, Frank told him the latest news. "We might have found Heinz-Erich Lüdemann, Dad," he said. He gave his father a shortened version of the personal ad they had placed in *Die Zeit*. "It turns out that somebody on the newspaper staff called this woman even before the ad printed, and now she wants to talk to us. Isabel is going to drive us to the restaurant."

"I'm impressed with your detective work," Fenton Hardy said proudly. "You seem to have this well under control."

"I guess we'll know more after we talk to the woman, Dad," Frank said. "We'll call you as soon as we get back."

Frank and Joe dressed for dinner in a nice restaurant and then headed downstairs to wait for Isabel. As usual, she was right on time.

"How do you do it, Isabel? Once again you're here on the dot," Joe said, climbing into her sports car. "I'm always either a few minutes ahead of time or a few minutes late."

Isabel grinned. "I just know how long it's going to take me to get to places in Lisbon," she said. She shrugged. "I never thought of it before."

After they got to Sua Excêlencia, parked Isabel's car, and walked through the front door of the restaurant, Joe glanced down at his watch. "Wow— on time again!" he said.

Isabel laughed. "Don't tell me that was a test!"

"No, I'm just trying to figure out what the secret is to being on time," Joe said, smiling.

Frank told the maître d' that they were meeting the party seated under the name "Santana."

"Ah, yes," the maître d' said. "This way, please."

The three of them began to follow him into the main room of the restaurant. They had gone no more than a few feet, though, when the maître d' stopped.

"What's wrong?" Frank asked.

"Well, that's Senhora Santana over there," the maître d' said, pointing, "but I don't understand why she's leaving with those men."

Joe looked. A woman with dark black hair was being led toward the rear of the restaurant by two men. "Frank—it's Captain Matos!" he said. "I don't recognize the other man."

"It doesn't matter. They're trying to kidnap Senhora Santana," Frank said. "Come on!"

The three of them raced toward the back of the restaurant, but Captain Matos had seen them. Now he and the other man were almost dragging Senhora Santana with them. They crashed through the swinging doors that led to the kitchen and disappeared.

Frank and Joe sped up.

When the Hardy boys and Isabel reached the kitchen, they found several overturned tables and trays of food—obviously meant to slow them down. When they got to the back of the kitchen, they saw an open side door. They raced toward it and saw that it led to a rear parking lot. A vehicle just like the one that Captain Matos used to shuttle the teens back to their hotel the other day was now speeding away.

"This parking lot will lead them back to the street in front," Isabel said. "If we hurry, we won't be too far behind."

Once again they raced back through the restaurant. There was still so much turmoil inside that nobody bothered to stop them and ask what was happening.

Just as they got outside Captain Matos's car was coming up the side of the restaurant. The Hardy boys and Isabel raced toward her sports car. They were in the car and on the street before Captain Matos's car had reached the corner of the block.

"This car can go twice as fast as that thing," Isabel said proudly. "They'll never get away from us!"

But it turned out to be harder than any of them thought it would be to keep up. Captain Matos's car raced through the narrow streets of Lisbon.

"Who is this Captain Matos?" Isabel asked.

"River police. We think he's also a member of one of the fascist groups," Joe said. "He's in on this in some way. He knew where our hotel was without our telling him."

Isabel shook her head. "My father would not believe this," she said, "because no one has ever been able to prove anything about police involvement in those fascist groups."

"That may change," Frank said.

"That guy could show the race-car drivers back home a thing or two," Joe said, keeping his eyes on the other car.

"That's the truth," Frank said. He looked over at Isabel. "Do you have your cell phone with you? We could get the police to set up some road blocks."

Isabel shook her head. "My phone needed to be charged and I didn't have time to do it."

"They're pulling ahead of us," Joe said.

Frank looked. The taillights of Captain Matos's car seemed to be getting smaller.

"Watch this!" Isabel said.

She shifted and the car shot forward. The size of the taillights quickly increased.

"Where are they headed?" Joe asked.

"Across the river," Isabel said. "We're almost to the Ponte 25 de Abril."

As she spoke the huge bridge came into view. It was brilliantly lit. Captain Matos's car was already on the bridge. By the time the Hardy boys and

Isabel reached the first span, Captain Matos's car was halfway across.

"We can't lose them, Isabel," Frank said. "If we do, then . . ."

Frank's jaw suddenly dropped midsentence. "Whoa. I don't believe it. Look!"

Up ahead, as if in slow motion, Captain Matos's car spun out of control. Suddenly it flipped over on its side and then tumbled end over end until it flipped over one of the guardrails and plunged into the Tagus River.

It took Isabel just a few minutes to reach the scene of the accident.

Joe jumped out and raced to the edge of the bridge. Down below he could still see one of the car's headlights, but he could tell that the car was sinking fast.

Other cars on the bridge had also pulled over to see the accident.

Joe began to take off his shoes.

"What do you think you're doing?" Frank demanded.

"I'm going in after Senhora Santana," Joe replied. "This is all our fault. We can't let her drown!"

"Joe," Frank said, "I don't think . . ."

"I'll be just fine, Frank," Joe said.

Joe got as close to the edge of the bridge as he could, took a deep breath, and plunged into the river.

The rescue mission seemed to take forever. Joe steeled himself against the impact of the water. Just as he hit the surface he held his arms over his head and totally relaxed his body, allowing it to plunge as far as the force of his entry would take it. The minute he felt pressure in his ears, he got ready to spring up. He suddenly forced himself upward and broke the surface of the river.

Joe opened his eyes and looked up toward the bridge. He waved at Frank and Isabel.

Frank let out the breath he had been holding.

"Amazing," Isabel said.

"It was an Olympic-quality dive," Frank said. "I hope he can repeat it the next time he competes back in Bayport."

"Too bad there were no judges around to give him a score," Isabel said.

Joe was swimming furiously toward Captain Matos's car. It was now totally submerged, but its headlights were still on.

When he finally reached the car, he took a deep breath and dove underwater.

Joe was amazed at how well the headlights illuminated the water around the car. Now he could see that the interior was also illuminated. Someone must have turned on the dome light either before or after the car hit the water. Joe wondered who it had been.

When he reached the side of the car, he saw

Senhora Santana's face at the window. She was clearly terrified.

He quickly gave her the hand signal for "okay," hoping that it had a universal meaning. It seemed to work.

Joe took a quick look inside the car. He was sure Captain Matos and the other man were dead.

Joe motioned Senhora Santana away from the window. He tried to smash the glass with the heel of his hand, but it wouldn't break. Inside, he saw Senhora Santana take a deep breath. All of a sudden the window started to lower. Joe realized that in this older-model car, the windows could be lowered manually. Senhora Santana was able to roll the window down only halfway before the pressure of the water cracked it, sending broken glass at both her and Joe.

Joe was sure that his chest was going to burst if he didn't surface soon—but he reached inside, grasped Senhora Santana's arms, and started to pull her out of the car.

Once he'd extracted Senhora Santana from the car, Joe put his arm around her waist and fought his way to the river's surface. Miraculously Senhora Santana was still breathing. She was unable to swim on her own, though, so after treading water for a few seconds Joe held her and swam with her toward the bank.

Frank and Isabel cheered. They had been joined on the bridge by several hundred other drivers who had been watching the drama unfold below them.

Two police vehicles had been summoned to the scene by drivers with cell phones. They were there in time to help pull Joe and Senhora Santana from the river.

"Come on," Isabel shouted. "We need to go meet them!"

Frank and Isabel jumped back into Isabel's car.

Just beyond the first span of the bridge there was a dirt road that had been built recently by a dredging company so it could get its equipment into the river. The police vehicles had taken that road and Isabel followed.

One of the police cars had a searchlight that was now scanning the river for Joe and Senhora Santana. Within seconds it landed on them.

Frank could see that one of the police officers was swimming in the river, heading toward Joe and Senhora Santana. When the policeman reached Joe, he took Senhora Santana and the three of them swam toward the bank.

As Joe reached the bank, his brother grabbed his hand.

"I could have made it," Joe said. "I was a little winded, but still, I could have made it."

"We know that," Isabel said. "And I will definitely be there for your Olympic performance!"

Joe grinned.

Another police officer handed a blanket to Joe. "Thanks," he said. He turned back to Frank and Isabel. "You're not going to believe Senhora Santana's story," he said. "She whispered some of it during our swim—it's incredible. And I've only really heard the *beginning* of it."

15 The Secret Revealed

Once on land Senhora Santana was given first aid and was pronounced to be in miraculously good condition given what she had just been through. She insisted that she didn't need to go to the hospital, and the doctor who examined her agreed.

"I must tell my story immediately," Senhora Santana said. "My grandfather could be in trouble now that these dangerous people know about the gold."

Frank looked at Isabel. "We're not far from your house," he said. "Your father probably needs to hear this too."

As Isabel's sports car barely held three people, they all decided that Joe would ride to Inspector Oliveira's house with Isabel and that Frank would ride with Senhora Santana in one of the police vehicles. The trip took only about fifteen minutes.

Inspector Oliveira met them at the door to the house. "Your father is on the telephone," he told the Hardy boys. "He sounds quite worried."

Joe took the call. "We're fine, Dad," he said. "And I think we've just about solved the mystery."

It turned out that Mr. and Mrs. Hardy and Aunt Gertrude had been watching television and saw a segment on the trouble at Sua Excêlencia. A reporter with one of Lisbon's television stations had been having dinner with his cameraman at the restaurant, and he was able to get some great shots—including one of the Hardy boys running through the restaurant toward the kitchen door.

"We didn't know what to think," Fenton Hardy said.

"We'll fill you in on everything when we get back to the hotel, Dad," Joe said. "I need to go now. Don't worry. I'm sure a police officer will bring us back. What could be safer than that?" He winked at Frank.

While Joe finished the call, Senhora Santana changed into some dry clothes that Isabel had managed to find. Once Joe hung up, he dried off and changed into some clothes borrowed from the inspector.

The Oliveiras' cook had made everyone some strong Portuguese coffee.

"Do you feel like talking now, Senhora Santana?" Inspector Oliveira said.

Senhora Santana nodded. "My grandfather has been waiting almost sixty years to return the gold to the Fleissners," she began. "He's now an old man. He had almost given up! I think now he can finally die in peace."

"Is he ill?" Frank asked.

"He isn't ill physically, really," Senhora Santana said, "but emotionally and spiritually, well—that's another story."

"It's a story I've heard often," Inspector Oliveira said. "The war had such an effect on millions of people."

Senhora Santana nodded. "Heinz-Erich Lüdemann didn't die. He was able to escape after the Gestapo took him back to Germany. He was on the run for almost two years—until the war was over. He hid in the forests, often just one step ahead of the authorities.

"After the war he returned to Lisbon, hoping to make contact again with the Fleissners. But he learned from Senhora Bragança that the Fleissners had fled to the United States. My grandfather entrusted Senhora Bragança with his secret and she let him dig up the suitcase from her garden. It was she, he told me, who suggested that he fill it with bricks and bury it again, which would throw off anyone who might come looking for it in the future."

Frank and Joe looked at each other.

"Exactly," Joe said.

"If anyone learned of the suitcase's existence and found it," Frank added, "whomever it was might just think that the bricks were what was buried in the first place, and that the gold had always been somewhere else."

Senhora Santana nodded. "With the end of the war and with so many displaced people moving themselves and their belongings around, nobody really thought much about the gold. It was actually quite common for people to dig up the wealth they had buried before and during the war and to carry it around with them. Heinz-Erich was one of many.

"Grandfather deposited the Fleissners' half of the gold in the largest bank in Lisbon. He put half of his half in another bank and then gave the rest to various relief agencies and other organizations who were trying to rebuild the lives of people who had lost everything."

"Your grandfather sounds like a remarkable man," Joe said. "I'd be honored to meet him."

"I think he'd like to meet the people who saved his granddaughter's life," Senhora Santana said. She turned to Frank and Isabel. "I'm including you in that," she added.

"We'd be honored too," Frank and Isabel said.

"There's something I still don't understand,

though," Joe said. "Throughout Europe, there's no record of a Heinz-Erich Lüdemann who would be the age of your grandfather. Did he change his name?"

Senhora Santana nodded. "After my grandfather's return to Portugal he sensed almost immediately that it would be best for him assume a new identity," she said. "He legally changed his name to Francisco Antunes and married a Portuguese girl—my grandmother.

"Over the years he discreetly tried to locate the Fleissners. He didn't want to be too public about it. He feared for his life. We heard stories of reprisals from ex-Nazis, not only in Europe but also in America." She looked directly at Frank and Joe. "The Nazis who fled after the war didn't just go to South America—they went to North America, too. My grandfather feared not only for his safety but also for the safety of the Fleissners. It's easy to think that he should have been bolder in his attempts, I know, and my mother and I often suggested it because it troubled him so—but we hadn't experienced what he had gone through, hiding for over two years and afraid of his own shadow. I can hardly imagine his fear. We offered to help him with the search—even to go to the United States ourselves—if it would bring him some peace, but he would never let us."

"It was just a guess on our part that he—or

someone who knew him—would see the personal ad that we placed in the German newspaper," Joe said.

"My grandfather taught my mother German and my mother taught me," Senhora Santana said. "No matter what happened during those horrible years, my grandfather was always proud of his German heritage."

Frank looked at Inspector Oliveira. "Now what?" he said.

"There should be no problem whatsoever," Inspector Oliveira said. "Frau Rilke will probably just need to prove that she is indeed the daughter of the Fleissners, and then the money will be hers."

"It's a fortune!" Senhora Santana said.

"Why don't you call her from here?" Isabel said. "It shouldn't be too late in the States."

Joe looked at his watch and calculated the time. "Well, even if she is in bed, I'm sure she won't mind being woken up for this news." It turned out that Frau Rilke *had* gone to bed, but she hadn't gone to sleep. In fact, she told Joe, she hadn't slept much since his last telephone call, when he had asked for the name of the German soldier.

"We found him under a different name," Joe said into the phone. "He's still alive and living in Lisbon." Joe heard a sob on the other end of the line. "After the war he put the gold bars in a bank here in Lisbon under your family's name. There's a fortune here for you."

With that news Frau Rilke said that she was so overcome with joy that she could no longer talk to Joe. Now that the gold had been found, she said that she would tell her family, and she asked Joe that he give the news to the daughter who lived with her. Frau Rilke passed the phone to her daughter, who greeted Joe. When he told her the news, he heard a clattering noise, as if the receiver had fallen to the floor. In the background, though, he heard what he could only describe as sounds of pure joy.

Joe waited for a minute. When no one picked up the receiver, he hung up. "We'll call back after we get to the hotel," he said with a grin. "Maybe by then someone will remember that we're on the phone!"

Two days later Frank and Joe, along with Mr. Hardy and Inspector Oliveira, met Frau Rilke and her daughter Heidi at the Lisbon airport.

On the drive into town, heading to the bank where Frau Rilke's account had been for over sixty years, Frank and Joe told them everything that had happened.

Some of the story, especially the part about jumping off the bridge to save Senhora Santana, even Fenton Hardy hadn't heard yet—and Joe noticed the proud look on their father's face.

Once they reached the bank Frau Rilke produced the necessary evidence to prove her identity. Inspector Oliveira had agreed to vouch for her as well. With the stroke of a computer key the Lisbon bank transferred the fortune they'd been holding for Frau Rilke into her account in Bayport.

"The secret of the soldier's gold has been solved!" Joe said.

"Yes, and the Hardy boys solved it," Frau Rilke said. She gave each boy a big hug. "I haven't forgotten my promise, either," she added. "Part of this money belongs to you."

Frau Rilke's daughter nodded. "Mother told me what she had promised to you, and she was right to do that," Heidi said. "Believe me—this is more money than we could ever use."

Frank and Joe looked at each other.

"Honestly, Frau Rilke, we couldn't take the money for ourselves," Frank said, "but I'm sure Joe would agree that it could really do Bayport High School some good."

"That's a wonderful suggestion," Frau Rilke said. "When we get back to Bayport we'll talk to the principal and find out what he's been putting off buying for the school because he hasn't had enough money."

Mr. Hardy looked at his watch. "We'll need to continue this discussion on the plane," he said. "We're all booked on the same flight back to New York."

"We'll stop by the hotel to pick up Mrs. Hardy, Aunt Gertrude, and everyone's luggage," Inspector Oliveira said, "and we'll rush everybody to the airport." He looked at Frank and Joe. "Isabel said to tell you two good-bye, but that she'll call you when she gets to Hollywood."

"Great!" Frank and Joe said.

Frau Rilke had another surprise for everyone. She and her daughter had actually decided to stay in Lisbon for two more days so they could have a short reunion with Heinz-Erich Lüdemann.

Everyone agreed that would be a perfect ending to the story. Inspector Oliveira said he'd be happy to help them get to wherever they needed to be.

As they left the bank Joe said, "Bayport High School is just about to become one of the most envied schools in the country."

"You're telling me," Frank said. "When we return, the school will be a lot richer—in both money *and* diving talent!"

Test your detective skills with these spine-tingling Aladdin Mysteries!

The Star-Spangled Secret
By K. M. Kimball

Mystery at Kittiwake Bay
By Joyce Stengel

Scared Stiff
By Willo Davis Roberts

O'Dwyer & Grady
Starring in Acting Innocent
By Eileen Heyes

Ghosts in the Gallery
By Barbara Brooks Wallace

The York Trilogy By Phyllis Reynolds Naylor

Shadows on the Wall

Faces in the Water

Footprints at the Window